UTOPIA PR

UTOPIA PR

ADAM BENDER

ISBN-13: 978-1-7360962-0-8 (*Paperback edition*)
ISBN-13: 978-1-7360962-1-5 (*eBook edition*)

Edited by Jim Spivey
Cover design by Bailey McGinn
Interior design by Phillip Gessert

UtopiaPR.info

Twitter: @Utopia_PR

For Rishi and Mallika, whose laughter and bright smiles lighten up the darkest days. Special thanks to Mom and Dad for all the silliness growing up.

PART
ONE

T HE GLOW OF fluorescent streetlamps was the only light as I squinted through cracked blinds at the early morning world outside the window. Two stories down, in front of our town house on Dogwood Lane, a black limousine waited.

Grumbling, I asked the dark sky, "What the heck is it this time?"

"Blake...?" asked my waking wife, looking peaceful and warm beneath the covers. It took all my willpower not to slip back into bed.

"I've got to go into work," I whispered, kissing her forehead. "Sorry, go back to sleep."

She mumbled something incomprehensible and drifted off. I released the blinds' aluminum slats and the bedroom snapped to black. Using my phone as a flash-light, I managed to find a pair of khakis on the closet floor and a mostly clean button-down in the laundry basket. I felt reassured that my blazer would hide my wrinkled sleeves, but the pants were old and kind of a squeeze.

I kissed my love again and headed down to the first floor. I couldn't find my winter coat anywhere and was already two steps back up the stairs to look for it when I saw the thing crumpled in a ball on the sofa. I put it on, went outside, and tapped my phone to lock the door.

As soon as my phone reentered my pocket, I realized I'd forgotten my work bag. With a short wave to the limo, I unlocked the door and went back inside. A few quick laps around the living room led me to the olive messenger bag sitting on the piano bench. I groaned to see a stain on the bag's bottom; it smelled of sweet raspberries. Oh well...there wasn't time to worry about that.

I locked up again and gave the door a good shake to make sure my phone had done its job. So as not to waste any more time, I clipped my government ID card to my belt while trotting toward the limo.

Warm air rushed into my face as I opened the car's door. Sinking into the creamy leather backseat, I let out a heavy sigh. Made it. I felt a queasy weightlessness as the wheels lifted into the undercarriage and the car lifted two feet above the ground.

"Your socks don't match," criticized a thin, Asian-American woman sitting across from me, as the hover limo whisked me away from my cozy townhouse. She was attractive in a praying mantis kind of way. While she was just a young intern, she wore a tailored, pin-striped suit that looked more expensive than my entire work wardrobe. I was pretty sure her name started with a *V*. Veronica?

"It's intentional," I said without checking the socks. "I'm testing your observational skills, which as you know are critical in public relations."

"My powers of observation also say you didn't shower."

"I didn't get to brush my teeth, either," I complained

while using a couple fingers to comb my greasy hair. "Did I have time?"

"No." She—Vanessa, maybe?—gave me that eyebrow-raised smile young people give to out-of-touch elders. Did she think I was old? I'm only thirty-five! And what's she? Twenty-five? It wasn't really a big age difference.

The hover limo increased velocity until my neighborhood was a blur. I felt like throwing up. My mind said it was a good thing I skipped breakfast, though my stomach didn't agree.

"Hey, what's the rush, anyway?" I asked.

The intern's expression turned grave. "One of Our Leader's hounds got loose."

"Oh," I said, taking this in. "TGIF."

Just another morning in Washington.

The hound isn't really a dog. Sure, it runs on four legs and has pointy ears like a Doberman, but it's actually a machine. The thing's coated in polished steel and wields a mouthful of sharpened razors. Our Leader's scientists designed the hound to protect the Compound and kill any would-be intruders.

Virginia, or whatever her name was, told me how the thing had jumped the fence of the Compound and made a break for it into Embassy Row—a wealthy neighborhood where a lot of diplomats used to live, back before Our Leader sent them packing. It was a nice place; my wife and I had thought about moving there, but we ended up deciding it was a little too close to work.

"Any vics?" I asked in the mode of a TV detective.

"Two." She handed me a tablet with video footage from neighborhood surveillance cameras.

I couldn't believe anyone would be up so early, especially with the outside temperature near freezing. Leave it to the physically fit to break all rules of rationality. In this case, they were a thirty-something jogger and a middle-aged power walker.

The jogger never saw the hound coming. Like a cheetah, the steel creature had burst from the shrubs and sprang ferociously toward her throat. The woman was dead before she knew what had mauled her.

The power-walking guy witnessed the attack from about fifty feet down the street. Surveillance showed him dropping his weights and sprinting the other way, but I guess the clang of the barbells against the pavement got the thing's attention. The mechanical beast bolted toward the walker at sixty miles per hour. It then pounced, claws extended, and slammed him into the asphalt.

"Cripes," I commented.

"Cripes?" repeated the intern in disbelief. "You watched that fucking shit, and all you can say is *cripes*?"

I waggled a finger at her. "You're here to learn, right? Well, here's your PR lesson for the day: Never curse. Not at work, not at home. Never. Because if you get too much in the habit, it might slip out in front of the microphone. Do you know how many PR reps have lost their jobs by blurting out profanity?"

She rolled her eyes. "What if you're too bottled up? You might explode one day."

Choosing not to be provoked further, I returned my gaze to the video on the tablet. The mechanical beast was still chewing on the man's face when the Hound Handlers showed up. They zapped the hound into stasis, zipped it into a burlap sack, then tossed the bundle into an unmarked white van to be returned to the Compound. A cleanup crew arrived to take the bodies and wash the blood off the street.

Strangely, I had a sudden craving for a jelly donut.

"You're still wearing the old badge," the intern said as she took back the tablet. "Security's not going to take it."

My eyes shot to the red ID fastened to my belt. The new one was blue, and I'd picked up mine last week but didn't remember what I'd done with it. Panicked, I flipped open my bag and dug through an impressive stash of empty soda bottles and candy bar wrappers. I could sense the judgmental youth raising her eyebrows at me again, but I soldiered on. Finally, the blue badge materialized inside a secret inside pocket that heretofore hadn't existed. Relieved, I switched out the IDs.

"Perhaps you have a matching sock in there, too?"

"Shut up, Vivian."

She scowled. That was the wrong name.

"Vanessa?"

So was that, and now the intern bared her teeth.

"Veronica? No, wait, don't tell me—"

"Vic—"

"Victoria Chu!" I exclaimed, cleverly throwing in the last name to prove that this was all a joke and in fact I had known her entire name all along.

Hoping to avoid further awkwardness, I gave my new ID an extra close inspection. In fact, I hadn't really looked at my new picture before, but here in the car, I saw it was a big downgrade from the one that had been on the red card. My cheeks looked chubbier, my hair looked unkempt, and—to top it all off—I'd forgotten to smile.

At the security gate to Our Leader's Compound, I had to flash my blue badge and send my bag through a metal detector. The concrete manor and military base made for a pretty big eyesore. I had much preferred the residence where Our Leader began his presidency, but he'd insisted it wasn't big enough and ordered the construction of this new Compound on his first day in office. A building can go up pretty quickly if the President declares its construction a national emergency. We moved in just under a year later.

Victoria and I walked up the long path to the main entrance. A wintry gust shook the cube-cut hedges and sent a chill right through the wool of my coat. There hadn't been any snow yet, but something in the air told me it was coming.

A burst of heat welcomed us inside. While true that the building's concrete and steel lacked the warm aesthetic of the old place, its central air truly was superior to the plug-in units we'd had to use there. I stopped to warm my hands on one particularly large vent, but Victoria whisked me down the hall to the Comms Situation Room.

Yes, I know the Comms Situation Room sounds important, but really, it's just an ordinary conference room. Its central feature is a big round table with a high-back mesh chair for each member of the communications team. There were large screens on all four walls. Generally, we used one for presentations, and a second to constantly play the National News Network, more commonly known as "Triple N." The other two displayed mystifying screen savers.

When I entered the room, the first screen displayed a blood-splashed slideshow of the hound, crimson eyes gleaming through horrific carnage.

Sitting around the table on laptops were Communications Director Scott Jones and Press Secretary Rico Fuentes. Rico sighed morosely, but good old Scott cheered my arrival: "Hey, hey, here comes the Hammer!"

The "Hammer" is me: Blake Hamner—the *n* is silent. I'm the government's go-to guy whenever things go way south. Because while Our Leader certainly knows how to control the people with an iron fist, he's not great at keeping up a friendly public image. I worked on his election campaign, and I like to think it's thanks to me that the people actually *chose* the whiny bastard to lead. Naturally, the new government asked me to stay on after the election to serve as Communications Director, but I knew I'd be bored with the day-to-day nonsense like taking pictures of Our Leader eating ice cream. So, I let my buddy Scott take the job with the understanding that he'd create a special role for me: Crisis Communications Manager. The idea was that they'd call me in to finesse the worst PR disasters. And to be clear, that's not a part-time role in this administration.

The stress lines around Scott's eyes showed me I'd made the right choice. All those ice-cream photos had left him looking positively refried. There was this thing that happened to his hair. He'd gone bald on top, but the poor guy never had any time to go to the barber, so the hair on the back and sides of his head had just kept getting longer. Now it looked like a wig slipping off the back of his head. I sometimes fantasized about grabbing hold of all that scruff and tugging it back up.

Rico seemed to be deteriorating, too. He was a young guy we'd hired to be our public face and point man with the media. Rico's pearly whites contrasted handsomely with his dark, carefully coiffed hair, and he understood the magic of a tailored suit. In front of the cameras, he carried the winning personality of a TV game show host. Behind the scenes, however, it was more like the losing personality of a disgruntled actor who wanted to do something—anything—other than host TV game shows.

I took my seat at the round table. Victoria plunked a mug of coffee in front of me. "Oh!" I called after her. "And a jelly donut!"

But she was already gone.

"Some intern," I grumbled.

"A donut's the last thing you need, Blake," said Rico.

Scott chuckled. "I wouldn't worry about refined sugar. It's the job that's gonna give us all heart attacks."

I smirked. "And a good morning to you both as well."

"Morning?" asked Scott, checking his watch with disbelief. "Oh fuck, it is morning. Fuck me dead, Blake. Fuck me dead on this very table."

I chose not to query if that meant he wanted to be screwed until or while he was dead. Instead, I asked how the hound got loose.

Scott shrugged. "They're doing some repairs on the fence. Apparently, the workers left a cherry picker out and the thing managed to climb it."

"You mean the fence is all that's keeping the hounds inside? Couldn't those idiots have programmed them not to leave the area?"

Scott swirled the coffee in his hand. "Our Leader didn't want to constrain their boundaries."

"So...what? Those things just roam around, killing everyone they see?"

"Smell," corrected Rico. "The eyes are decoration."

"They won't kill everyone," added Scott. "Just anyone without Compound access."

"So," I said, shaking my head in disbelief, "everyone."

We had one hour to figure out a plausible explanation to give the media for the hound's rampage in Embassy Row.

Not every PR rep gets this, but the media is an important ally. Most people don't trust people in power, whether it's the government or a big corporation. All the "everything is great" press releases in the world aren't going to change that. Too much good news might actually increase people's suspicions. Better for the news to come from Triple N's star anchor Maria Worthington, who speaks to viewers as if they're sitting together at the city's coziest café.

"Mm," I murmured, picturing Maria's cinnamon-brown hand as it brings a hot cappuccino to her sultry lips.

Scott shook me. "Blake? Blake? Are you there, Blake?"

I opened my eyes. "I was just thinking."

"We are fucked," grumbled Rico, tugging his ID card

about a foot out from its retractable holder and letting it snap back to punctuate the sentence.

I scowled. Rico was becoming a really crappy Press Secretary. A PR flack has got to maintain some level of optimism. He can totally be a cynic—seriously, I'm fine with that—but pessimism just holds back the imagination. Rico started this job bright-eyed and bushy-tailed, but now was behaving like a diseased donkey.

"You need to cool it with the profanity, Rico," I reprimanded, then turned to the Communications Director. "You, too, Scott."

"You'll have to excuse us," the older colleague said. "We didn't get to go home yesterday because of the Annual Late-December Holiday Celebration."

I didn't go to the state dinner, though I appreciated Our Leader's progressive effort to be inclusive of all religions. My father is half-Jewish, half-Buddhist, while my mother is half-Christian, one-quarter Muslim, and one-quarter Hindu. In what I consider a stroke of pure brilliance, I synthesized all these contradictions into a single belief system known as atheism.

Scott continued. "We had a prepared speech in which Our Leader was going to formally forgive everyone who didn't vote for him, but instead he spent his full twenty minutes tearing a new asshole out of Funnyman Dan for that monologue he did Wednesday night."

My favorite late-night host had been ribbing Our Leader for months, but earlier this week he had apparently hit a nerve with a joke about the President's steady weight gain since taking office. "No wonder there's no First Lady," Dan had joked. "She'd have no room in bed!"

"I had a fucking lot of Merlot, followed by a fucking

lot of coffee," Scott said. "I thought they'd balance each other out. They didn't. I'm not even sure I'm really awake."

I decided that their night sounded awful enough for me to let the cursing slide this time. "Oh, you're not dreaming," I chirped, running a hand through my full head of hair. "I am actually this handsome in real life."

"How are you so fucking positive?" Rico growled. "You know I haven't stepped outside the Compound for an entire week? I haven't even had time to get my new ID card. My partner dumped me by text yesterday, claiming I wasn't putting any effort into our relationship!"

"What did you say?" asked Scott with concern.

"I haven't replied yet."

The Communications Director's eyes blinked with disbelief.

Since I didn't care about Rico's love life, I changed the subject. "What do we know about the victims? Surely there's some dirt to be found."

Scott pulled up the file on the jogger. "Lawyer, thirty-seven years old, divorced, no children..."

"I said *dirt*, not her life story."

Scott scrolled down to a category labeled *Questionable Activities*. The government had flagged a few concerning library borrows—books about criminal justice—but it didn't seem too shocking of a list for an attorney. Her recent credit card transactions looked more promising. She'd recently donated money to Jason Stonybrook, the conservative who'd run against Our Leader in the last election.

Scott clapped appreciatively. "OK, and what about the power walker?"

We didn't have to scroll long to find a questionable enough activity. Scott and I shot up from our seats and chanted the words on the screen: "Disgraced pedophile priest! Disgraced pedophile priest! Disgraced pedophile priest!"

"I had one of those growing up," commented Rico, killing the mood as usual. Scott and I lowered our arms and sat down. Miserably, the Press Secretary asked, "What about neighborhood witnesses to the attack? Won't we have to discredit them, too?"

I wouldn't let Rico's grumpiness derail me. "Most people were sleeping, right? A few might have seen the Handlers cleaning up, but it was still dark, so they'll be hazy on what actually happened. That means they'll buy a good story."

Rico blinked. "You really think we can *spin* this?"

"Maybe you see a vicious killing machine that got loose and went on a rampage, but I sure don't. No, I see a hound who, minding her own business inside our compound, sniffed out two highly questionable people and took initiative to save the day!" I pointed to the photo of the blood-soaked beast. "Why, that there is a *Hero Pup*!"

Scott didn't look convinced. "I admit that sounds fucking *cute*, but c'mon, that thing looks like a monster."

"No," I said, "she looks like a monster *now*."

CHAPTER
TWO

W ITH ABOUT FIVE minutes to spare, we sent the media an invitation to a press conference. We placed an embargo on any reporting about what had happened ahead of the announcement, and timed the press conference to begin just as Maria Worthington went on the air, forcing Triple N to cut straight to the live event without giving the beautiful anchor any time to try to explain what had happened. Sorry, Maria.

Even though it was a little cold, we decided to hold the event in the Rose Garden. We had poinsettias, wreathes, and other holiday arrangements up. Scott and I stood shoulder-to-shoulder behind several rows of seated reporters. TV camera drones flitted back and forth overhead like hummingbirds, employing competing algorithms to calculate the optimal shot of the President.

It began with Our smilin' Leader standing with a leashed hound that looked the epitome of man's best friend. The President was a short, pudgy man with severe facial features, but an indigo turtleneck and gray blazer made him look powerful. Cameras flashed as he leaned toward the hound and attached a golden metal tag to its collar, which was powder-blue with white paw prints. Friendly purple light glowed from the machine's eye sockets.

"Oh, this is hashtag #beautiful," twittered Debbie Butters, tapping a smartphone as she spoke to send the comment to the masses. The middle-aged woman with an affinity for floral-patterned pantsuits was our Social Media Director. She was round and chirpy, like a digitally savvy robin, and she had a bad habit of sneaking up on me. I hadn't noticed she was standing with us until she spoke.

"What are you doing?" asked Scott.

"Woozing," she said.

"What?" he asked, horrified. "Do you need a Band-Aid?"

I explained to him for the hundredth time that *woozing* just meant posting on Woozler, our nation's top social network for the last few years.

"People are loving the Hero Pup," commented Debbie. "Literally. The love-to-like ratio is off the charts."

"Great!" I replied. I rarely knew what Debbie's statistics meant, so I usually responded based on her facial expression.

"We should have thought of this yesterday for the shoot," she prattled. "Victoria helped me do a little 'Meet the Hound Handlers' for social. She spent a lot of time helping them polish the little doggies so they'd look their best for the photos, but we certainly didn't think to dress them up! I haven't posted it yet, so maybe we should have a do-over with the new-and-improved Hero—"

"Shh!" I snapped. The President was starting to address the reporters.

"This heroic doggy brought quick, decisive justice to deviants," Our Leader proclaimed.

Scott whispered, "Can't believe you got him to say 'doggy.'"

I smirked. "That's why they pay me the big bucks."

Our Leader patted the monster on the head, prompting a speaker in the hound's mouth to emit a puppy woof.

The reporters cooed. Eager for a scoop, one asked the dog's name.

"Can we keep her?" another chimed in.

The crowd roared with laughter.

In my notebook I scrawled: *Naming contest?*

"Great idea!" burst Debbie, reading over my shoulder. "That would be perfect for social. Let me get right on that!" She ran off.

"Hey, guys," said a morose voice behind us. Rico, of course.

"Where the hell have you been?" asked Scott.

"Finally had a chance to take a dump."

I recoiled. "Jesus!"

He exhaled with relief. "You're telling me."

Shuddering, I turned back to the stage—and froze. The hound seemed to be sniffing the air, and I could swear it was looking right at me.

Our Leader continued his remarks. "We owe much to this mutt for her *sharp* endeavor, for her *voracious* savvy, and for her *unrelenting* patriotism."

Still chatting, Scott and Rico didn't notice the beast watching us. "Personally," Scott said, "I've been pissing brown all night."

"Uh, guys," I croaked. "Is that thing...?"

The hound launched itself from the stage. The reporters, apparently under the impression this was part of the show, *ooh*ed at the Hero Pup's athleticism. The camera drones whipped around to get a shot of the three of us just as Scott let out a girlish whimper and fainted. Rico flailed his arms and ran.

I just stood there.

The hound, *arf*-ing pleasantly, hit full speed and pounced.

They say images of your life flash before your eyes when you're about to die. All I could think of was my wife watching this on live TV. The cameras were pointed right at me as the hound lunged at my neck. I got a glimpse of its terrible teeth and shut my eyes.

Someone behind me let loose a high-pitched scream. Turning to look, I saw Rico sprawled on the grass with the thing gnashing its teeth on top of him. He tried to defend himself with his red ID card, fully extended from his belt retractor. Red—the old badge. Of course, the hound thought he was an intruder.

Before I could figure out how to save the idiot, the monster's body went limp. One of the Hound Handlers must have zapped it. Rico stopped screaming, began sobbing pathetically. The crowd of reporters moved curiously toward us until it was just me standing between them and the hound. Beyond their heads, I could see the deep scowl of Our Leader. This was bad. If I didn't come up with something fast, the royal bastard was liable to feed the entire comms staff to the hound. But how the heck could anyone spin this?

A woman laughed behind us, as if it was all some kind of joke. I turned and saw Victoria.

Addressing the reporters, she asked, "Playful girl, isn't

she?" She leaned over to rub the head of the sleeping hound. "Isn't she? Isn't she? Yes, she is! Yes, she is!"

Unsure, the reporters turned to Rico. And you know, as much as I've been bashing the man, I've got to give him some credit for his response. "This," the Press Secretary squeaked from beneath the machine, "is the cutest thing that's ever happened to me!"

Scott bolted upright from his faint as if it had never happened. "All right, folks, that's it! Thanks for coming out!"

Our Leader demanded that the entire communications team join him immediately in the Throne Room. The cavernous chamber featured marble columns that shot up from a scarlet carpet on the floor to a grand ceiling painted like the Sistine Chapel. But instead of God, the mural depicted the President in all his glory.

The five of us lined up before the President, who sat in his gold-trimmed and very plushy chair. So comfortable was the seat that Our Leader struggled to stand, and he had to call for one of the puffy-shirted guards to help him up. When he finally got onto his feet, Our Leader roared, "What a fucking disaster!"

"Everything turned out OK," I offered.

I could see a vein bulging in Our Leader's forehead. "Don't you try to clean this up, Hamner. You idiots nearly blew it after making me look like a sniveling puppy lover on TV! You know I fucking hate dogs!"

This was accurate, though I didn't know why. Maybe he got nipped by a Chihuahua as a child. Incidentally, I could never stop Our Leader from using profanity. There was no use trying.

Swiping furiously on her phone, Debbie offered, "Everyone on Woozler went ballistic over the Hero Pup, but sentiment swung wildly from *love*, to *surprised*, to *rolling on the floor laughing*, and then to *angry*."

I turned to our social guru. "Wait, when were they laughing and when were they angry?"

"Laughing when the hound attacked Rico. Angry when the hound was subdued. Victoria got a handful of likes for petting the poor thing."

I gasped. "*Poor* thing? It could have killed me! Or one of you!"

Rico spoke up. "It was my fault, sir. I didn't get a chance to pick up the new ID badge, and—"

"The hound should have torn you apart limb from limb," Our Leader stated grimly. "Guards, take away the Press Secretary."

Rico suddenly looked more awake than he had in hours. "What?! No, wait!"

Two guards took Rico by the arms and dragged him kicking and screaming. Worried about saving my own butt, I pretended not to hear his cries.

Our Leader cracked a smile and winked at Veronica.

"What's your name, baby?"

"Victoria," she replied coldly.

Oh right. Victoria.

Scott explained she was an intern, which seemed to impress Our Leader. "You did good saving these morons," he said. "Not sure they deserved it, but hey! So, intern no more. I'm making you Communications Director, baby."

"But that's my job," whimpered Scott.

"Not anymore," said Our Leader. "Hey, I know, why don't you be Vivian's assistant?"

"Deputy," suggested my former intern. "And it's Victoria."

"Deputy Communications Director," said the President. "Perfect."

"But-but," stammered Scott, "that's a demotion."

"And it will be up to Astoria—"

"Victoria," she corrected again.

"—to decide whether you have a job at all a month from now." Our Leader looked at me and added, "That goes for Blake, too."

"What about Debbie?" asked Scott, throwing her under the bus without a care.

The President shrugged. "Debbie's cool."

The social expert beamed. "Hashtag #thankful," she said.

Victoria, the intern who was now suddenly our boss, looked at Scott and me like a cat pondering what to do with a couple of baby bluebirds. "I do have some changes in mind," she purred.

I tried appealing to Our Leader's appreciation for loyalty. "Sir, all due respect, but we helped you win the election."

"Nonsense!" he declared. "I won all by myself. You were just there for the ride. It's me the people love, not you morons."

I decided to take a short break at Sarah's Diner. It was one of those old-fashioned breakfast joints with sea-foam tile, sparkling white booths, and chrome details. There was even a jukebox with actual vinyl records in the corner, though it had been out of service for as long as I could remember.

I chose my favorite spot to sit—at the counter, where there was a good view of the TV showing Triple N. Sarah poured me a cup of coffee and asked if I wanted a donut. The way she asked it sounded more like a statement of fact than a question.

"Give me the fattest you've got, bursting with jelly," I replied.

"So, the usual."

Sarah gets the best donuts in town. She selected one for me that was so big and sticky, I needed a fork and knife to attack it.

While I ate, I tried to focus on the news channel rather than think about the chewing out I'd just gotten from Our Leader. Maria Worthington ran the whole story about the hound as a puff piece. They even put on some goofy music when the thing attacked us, as if it was one of those silly home video shows.

"So there you have it, Maria," said a reporter standing outside the gates of the Compound. "A Hero Pup."

The image flashed over to a golden newsroom, where I became immediately lost in the anchor's lustrous black hair. "What, no interview with the dog?"

The reporter laughed. "I didn't have a dog whisperer with me."

Maria shook a fist in mock frustration. "Guess we'll have to hire one!"

I got a call from the wife a few minutes after the news ended. I licked the last bits of strawberry jam from my fingers, dried my hand on my suit pants, then picked up the phone.

"Maria, my love."

"Damn it, Blake, that hero dog nonsense was darn cute," she told me.

I grinned into the receiver. "What do you mean nonsense?"

"How about next time you give us an exclusive interview?"

"With the dog?"

"Yeah, Blake," she replied sarcastically. "With the dog."

"Sorry, no special privileges, remember?"

Maria and I have this rule—she doesn't ask me for inside information about my work, and I don't use our relationship as leverage on what she reports. They say you shouldn't keep things from each other in a marriage. Well, the only secrets between Maria and me are professional.

I sipped my coffee as my wife retorted, "Don't worry, I won't force you to breach ethics for a *poop scoop*."

Coffee sprayed from my mouth onto the counter. Sarah wrinkled her brow at me and got a towel.

"You're not at that diner again, are you?"

I could never figure out how she did this. Maria kept closer tabs on me than the government. "Maybe."

"Lay off the donuts, Blake. I promise they won't be offended."

"But..."

"Our Leader must be happy with you, though, right?"

I sighed. "Actually, he demoted Scott and threatened to take away my job. Also, Rico might be dead?"

Maria snickered; she must have thought I was joking. "You know what I thought when I saw you on TV?"

"That I looked fat?"

"No. Well, yes. But no. I thought, *Of course Blake's there*. This had your name written all over it. I mean, that hound killed two people—traitors, apparently, but they're still human beings."

"Yeah, I know."

"The crazy thing is, thanks to you, I actually want a dog now. Hey, Ham, do you think Our Leader has a spare hound we could adopt?"

I felt my grip on the phone tighten as my wife giggled evilly. Usually, I have the answer to everything. It's my job. But with Maria...well, she's the only one who knows how to leave me speechless.

CHAPTER
THREE

A LOT OF people—myself included—have at some point felt a little jealous of Maria and her career's seemingly meteoric rise, but the truth was she'd had to work her butt off. During her senior year at J-School, she snagged an internship at the National News Network. She was Triple N's only Black woman intern. She told me later that she had to work twice as hard as the other students to be taken seriously.

The unpaid position was anything but glamorous. Three days a week, she'd write some of the headlines that scrolled along the bottom of the screen during the 6:00 a.m. show. She simply wouldn't sleep the night before. The crew arrived a few hours before the show started, so there really was no point. She'd stay up all night, head into the office at about four thirty, work until about ten, then head straight to her first class. I assume she found some time to sleep in the afternoon.

Maria quickly showed Triple N that she had strong work ethic and smart news judgment. As soon as she graduated college, the cable network hired her for an on-camera gig interviewing people on the street. That's the reporter who goes up to randoms asking if they've ever seen so many crushed worms after a rainstorm before. It's not exactly interviewing the mayor, so few reporters put in the effort to really do it well. But man, Maria could turn those annelid pancakes into stars!

Two years later, Triple N asked her to become one of the co-anchors on the six-in-the-morning time slot for which she had originally interned. That may sound early, but a lot of people watch the news before they go to work. The promotion also got considerable buzz in a country where most TV anchors were white. While some celebrated Maria's achievement, others dismissed it as Triple N trying to look woke. Despite having to share the slot with a Caucasian male co-anchor, she actually got some hate mail—and even death threats. While her network bosses largely supported her, they still forced her to "look the part," for example by straightening her hair to look more "professional." Deciding to pick her battles, Maria did as she was told. And she worked even harder to prove herself.

She steadily increased her likability rating over the year until it was higher than anybody else's on the network. At peak popularity, Maria asked for and secured a late-morning slot. Going on at ten still required her to get to work at around eight, but she said the extra hours of sleep increased her job satisfaction immensely. What Maria may have lost in the commuter audience, she made up for with stay-at-home parents and freelancers pretending not to be unemployed.

Sorry, freelancers, that was a little harsh. Really, I was just talking about myself. See, I wanted to be a journalist, too, but I never found a way to make it pay the bills. Even though I went to the famous J-School at National University, and even though I scored a perfect 4.0 GPA, I struggled to get a job after graduation. Unlike Maria, my face is more suited to print journalism, so in my senior year I applied to various capital newspapers—revered old institutions like the *Capital Post* and vicious upstarts like *Politi-Go-Go*. But the furthest I ever got was a telephone interview.

The good news was that my parents had some money saved. So rather than become a barista or whatever, I started a political blog about the dumb flubs of politicians. I called it "The Hammer." I'd open each piece explaining who said what, with some context about why they might have said such a thing. Then I'd write a little analysis on how they could have avoided controversy and what they could say now to get them out of trouble. I put up a few sponsored ads from Woozle, but honestly didn't expect to make much dough in the beginning.

Things started to change when City Council member Donna Willikers gave a commencement speech at an arts college. She told the students that they would likely have no future and should seek a more important degree, like cybersecurity. Naturally, they booed her off the stage. After doing a little research, I learned that Willikers's son had a large-ish following on Woozler for a style of art he termed post-abstract, which looked a lot like realism. He was about seventeen, which meant he was probably thinking about where to go for college (if anywhere). So, in my blog, I explained that this could very well be fueling Willikers's attack on the arts. While she might never recover among the art community, I posited that they didn't represent as large of a voter bloc as worried parents of teenagers. There were probably a lot of parents who would agree with Willikers—maybe not her exact words, but the emotion behind them. So, I proposed that

Willikers turn her controversy into a policy—propose that art students be required to dual-major, or at least minor, in a STEM (Science, Technology, Engineering, and Mathematics) field.

That blog post got heaps of clicks. More amazingly, Willikers followed my advice. At first, I wrote that off as coincidence, figuring her paid PR staff probably reached the same obvious conclusion I had. But things like that began happening more and more, and before I knew it, people were asking *me* to advertise on my website. It wasn't a lot of money, but it was enough to keep me in my studio apartment.

A few years into the blog, I wrote about Senator Ron Brown, who had misspoken (he said) and accidentally (he said) used a racist slur on live TV. Everyone was in an uproar, with the media questioning what plausible excuse he could make that would make this go away.

I blogged that the solution was simple: just admit it was a mistake and say he was sorry. A lot of PR reps would never think of that because they view takebacks and apologies as weaknesses, but I'd say it's human.

That post got me a TV interview on Triple N. I was nervous, which I thought was because—you know—live TV, but when I sat down across from Maria Worthington, I realized it was because of her. To get ideas for my blog, I had watched a lot of Triple N. Many of the anchors felt like old friends even though I'd never met them. Five seconds before the cameras came on, I realized with terror that my feelings for Maria had become more like a crush.

Somehow, I got through the interview. More than that, Maria seemed genuinely impressed with my advising politicians to get over themselves and apologize. She even laughed at my jokes, and when she smiled, dimples formed on her cheeks that I'd never noticed through the TV screen.

There was still another thirty minutes left in her show, but I decided to stick around to try to talk to her afterward. I don't know what I was thinking. She could've had a boyfriend, or a husband, or three children. But I just couldn't leave.

And you know what, it wasn't even that hard. Maria said she wanted to ask me more about how to deal with flacks, which is what journalists called PR reps. I asked her if she wanted to talk more about public relations tactics over lunch.

If you were wondering, Senator Brown didn't follow my advice. Instead, he doubled down, insisting that what he had said wasn't racist and the fact that people thought it was racist proved that they were the real racists. A few days later, Brown was forced to resign.

I would have felt vindicated if I wasn't so distracted by my budding romance with Maria. I'd never experienced a relationship so effortless. We could talk about anything. She kept my sometimes-inflated ego in check, and I didn't even mind. We saw each other every chance we could get. On our two-year anniversary, I asked Maria to marry me.

We had the ceremony at a great big church in the city. Neither of us were religious, but Maria's mother was devout and won the argument. There was a big party afterward at the National News Museum with lots of booze, and frankly I don't remember much about it. We had wanted to go on a honeymoon at a tropical beach somewhere, but with Maria's job and intensifying demands from my advertisers to pump out the blog posts, we postponed the trip and went right back to work.

More years went by. We bought a house, mainly with Maria's paycheck, but she never made me feel bad about money. She'd tell me that people loved my blog and that it would lead to big things one day.

CHAPTER
FOUR

MARIA AND I went to dinner at Zand, a trendy new restaurant she had been wanting to try. I had my doubts from the moment I saw the menu, which asked us to choose a color rather than a meal. We had trouble choosing, so the waiter recommended we share a rainbow, as it was "perfect for couples."

The restaurant looked like someone had poured the sands of Dubai into a renovated old bank. Diamond chandeliers hanging from its high ceilings added to the uncertainty as to whether one was inside or out. I traced an ant-colony stream of waiters to a round opening that was once an old vault but now served as a kitchen.

"There can't be much ventilation in there," I commented. "Seems like a fire hazard."

"Only if you lock the chefs inside," returned Maria.

The quip nearly made me spit up my ice water. "I love you." It was all I could say sometimes.

My wife was looking gorgeous in an emerald green dress that draped nicely over her voluptuous curves. Since wrapping her news show, she'd accentuated her full lips with deep red lipstick and added shimmering eyeshadow that made her look like some unearthly goddess. The network was too conservative to let her look like this on camera; going out was Maria's time to let her truth shine.

It did make me feel a little guilty that I had come to the date as merely a mussier version of my morning self—which hadn't been that impressive to begin with. I hadn't even fixed my mismatched socks. Maybe this, I reflected, was my truth.

"But what do you think?" she asked. "Am I making too big a deal out of this?"

I blinked. Maria had been telling me something important for the last few minutes, but my mind had been elsewhere. "No, definitely not," said I, assuming it was the right answer.

"I'm just worried we're going to lose our independence," she said while shaking the ice in her neon-green cocktail.

I understood now that she was talking about her job. Triple N had just been acquired by Joe Steele. He was the CEO of Woozle, probably the country's biggest e-commerce firm. This wasn't the first time Maria had raised concerns about what that might mean for a free press.

"It could be worse," I offered with a wink. "You could be controlled by the government."

She laughed. "Steele was pretty outspoken against Our Leader in the last election, so I guess there's no danger of that." Maria shook her head. "Sometimes I think we both should quit, pack up, and get out of the capital."

"I want to, but..."

She waited for me to go on, but of course I didn't. I never knew how to finish that sentence, though the *but* usually was enough to end the conversation. At least it showed I was acknowledging her point.

The waiter arrived. Flourishing his wrist like a magician, he placed onto the table a tall glass pitcher containing several layers of colored sand.

"We already have a candle," I murmured.

The waiter dropped two twisting and curvaceous straws into the pitcher, carefully pointing the ends of each toward our respective mouths.

Maria giggled. "I think it's a drink."

"No, madame!" protested the mustachioed waiter. He was either very French or putting on an exaggerated accent. "It is *Zand*."

We returned his statement with blank stares.

Following a pompous sigh, our server brought himself to explain it was our entrée. Then he left us to it.

"Well," said Maria, "Linda at work said this place was good."

"Linda? Isn't she bulimic?"

"Hey now," scolded Maria. "We don't know for sure which specific eating disorder she has..."

I grinned. "Can you imagine what throwing up *Zand* would look like?"

Maria laughed mid-sip of the colored dust. Coughing the stuff onto the table, she reminded me of a kitten spitting up a hairball—gross, but still kind of cute. "Yeah, probably a lot like that," I remarked.

"We shouldn't joke about this stuff, Blake," she scolded, but I could tell she wasn't mad. "Besides, I think Linda's recovering. I caught her today with a bagel."

"Anything on it?"

"Cream cheese."

"Oh wow. How thin of a layer?"

She kicked me teasingly under the table. "Blake..."

Peering into the glass of rainbow powder, I asked, "What's it taste like, anyway? The candle."

Maria wiped her mouth with a napkin. "Do you remember Pixy Stix?"

"Ew."

"Like that, only savory."

I gagged.

"I'm not sure if it's... I'm not sure if it's beef? Or maybe some kind of fish?"

That seemed like a big enough difference to justify avoiding the entrée altogether, so I flicked away my straw.

Maria frowned. "Sorry, we can go for a burger after this."

"Yeah, maybe."

The truth was, I was getting tired of restaurants in general—not just the weird ones. I hated having to look nice just so I could stuff my face. And all the dang decisions! What wine pairs best with the salmon? Should we split an appetizer? Should we get dessert and coffee? Should we split one dessert? Or maybe we should skip dessert since we got the appetizer? Is it too late for coffee? It was all...so...exhausting.

Before I worked for Our Leader, I'd enjoyed cooking nice meals at home. In fact, on our third date, I made coq au vin. How did it come out? Well, Maria married me, didn't she?

Since I became Crisis Communications Manager, we mostly ate out, got delivery, or applied high heat to frozen pizza. The problem was neither of us had any energy left to cook when we got home from work. Even if I could find the strength to lift a frying pan from the cabinet, there would be nothing in the fridge for me to sauté. Who had time to go to the grocery store?

An older couple in coats lingered by our table. The lady stared at my wife and stammered, "Excuse me, I'm sorry, but are you, are you, Maria...Worthington? From the TV?"

Maria gave the woman her best Triple N smile. "Why, yes. Do you watch the program?"

The lady blushed. "Oh, I...I just think you're great. I'm sorry to interrupt your dinner, but I wanted to tell you that."

I remarked, "You're not the first and, I hate to say, you won't be the last." It got me a blank stare from the woman and a scowl from her husband.

"We'll be going, then," said the fan-lady, turning back to Maria. "It was good to meet you, Mrs. Worthington."

People always got that wrong. It was Ms. Worthington. It was not unlike how people always mispronounced my last name.

When the couple had gone, Maria scolded me. "You didn't have to be rude."

"What did I say?"

She raised her eyebrows.

"Sorry, I just don't like interruptions when we're out together."

She nodded as if she understood. Changing the subject, Maria asked, "How would you pitch this place, anyway?"

"Ooh," I replied giddily. This was a PR game we liked to play when we were somewhere awful: pretend you were being paid to say something nice.

Holding up my pointer finger, I declared, "A memorable experience—"

Maria snickered.

"—that will leave you wanting more. Much, much more."

Maria hooted, attracting irritated glances from other patrons. She looked embarrassed, but I told her not to worry: "They're just hangry."

I started thinking more about what she'd said about quitting our jobs and getting away from all this nonsense. I wanted to whisk her away to a tropical island, spending the days lounging on the beach and the nights—and that reminded me we still hadn't gotten around to our honeymoon.

"What's up, Ham? The Victoria thing?"

"Veronica," I corrected. "No wait, maybe you're right. I think it is Victoria." I shrugged and shook my head. "There's that, but also...this morning, I was looking at my old ID badge. I got that picture taken on Inauguration Day. I looked pretty good, actually. But now I just look stressed out—"

"Mm," agreed my wife. "And fat."

I knew she was making a joke, but the truth hurt all the same. "I don't know, I started thinking that maybe what I want to do is pack up and start my own little PR company. Take on some lighter jobs, you know? Maybe even have a little fun?"

I felt Maria's foot again, bare now, rubbing against my thigh. "I think it's a good idea."

My phone beeped—a text message from Scott:
Fuck me love.
Damn autocorrect.

Fuck my life.

"Let me guess—Scott?" asked Maria. I noticed she'd withdrawn her foot.

"Oh, he's pretty broken up about the demotion. I think he's drinking. I...I should really go check on him, make sure he's all right."

She frowned. "I thought we could go home, and, you know, think more about our future?"

My phone beeped again. This one, and I'm not sure how he got it past autocorrect, just said: *Fuuuuuuuccc-cckkkk!*

I grumbled.

"I thought you didn't like interruptions when we're out," she said.

"This is different. I'm a little worried about the guy."

"Fine," said Maria, reading my sullen face. "Go to him."

"I mean, we could both leave and get burgers on the way..."

She took another sip of the weird powder. "No, no. This is actually kind of growing on me. Get a burger with Scott, and then I'll see you at home. Just don't stay out too late, OK?"

The next thing I remember clearly is trying to pee off a sticker that someone had placed on the inside of a urinal. I'd seen this steampunk image of a dude in a jetpack before. Someone, or more likely a group of people, was putting these things up all around the city. For every decal the police took down, two more seemed to go up.

It was grassroots PR, and I didn't like it. But despite my minute-long outpouring of several drinks, the sticker failed to disintegrate from the porcelain wall.

As I turned on the faucet to wash my hands, an ad popped up on the mirror: *Hello, Blake Hammer! Buy 1 value pack of diapers, get the 2nd pack 25% off! This week only on the Woozle Marketplace.*

It always amazed me how smart and dumb technology could be at the same time. This one was smart in its use of facial recognition to identify me, but dumb in that it had spelled my last name wrong and because I didn't have a baby. The only explanation I could think of was that the advertisers had taken note of my years-ago wedding and made the false assumption that we would have started a family by now.

"Shut up, mirror." I swiped away the ad and took in a face with five-o'clock shadow. No amount of splashing was going to remove the bags from my eyes.

I rejoined Scott at the bar, where our enabler Mike was bringing two more glasses of Scotch and clearing a tower of empties. We clinked glasses and Scott downed his whiskey in a single gulp. Part of me still knew I was drinking too much, so I sipped mine.

"Maybe I should just fucking quit, you know?" Scott burbled.

"No," I said. "I'm telling you; you've just got to fight for it. Victoria's fresh. She doesn't know what she's doing. She'll fail and you'll get the job back."

"Shit, what's the point?"

"What else are you going to do? Roll over? This is your life, Scott."

Scott signaled Mike for another beverage. "She's gunning for you, too. Veronica, I mean."

"Victoria."

"Her, too," slurred Scott. "She wants to reshape the whole damn operation!" He squinted at my face as if he needed glasses. "You're not freaking out about that?"

I shrugged. "I don't know. To be honest, I've been thinking about leaving. Maybe I could start my own PR shop, set my own hours..."

Scott's jaw dropped. "I can't believe what I'm hearing! You can't leave!"

"This government stuff's not good for me, Scott. Maria thinks I'm fat, I'm tired all the time..."

"Then work out!" he shouted, blowing a Scotch-infused wind up my nostrils. "Try meditation!"

I shook my head. "When that hound jumped us today, I saw my life flash before my eyes."

"That's not a real thing! Don't bullshit me, Blake. I've been in PR too long not to know bullshit when I hear it. Dammit, Blake...you're the fucking Hammer, you know? You are. You are the fucking Hammer. You won us the fucking election. We're at the top of our careers!"

Perhaps seeing our misery, the bartender brought us two fresh glasses.

Scott shook his head. "All I'm saying is we can't let this intern swoop in and take away everything that we earned. We can quit later, but we can't let Victoria—"

"Veronica."

"I thought you said before it was Victoria?"

"Oh yeah. Maybe."

"All I'm saying is, we can't let her think we're just going to roll over like little bitches."

It sounded like a great point, probably because it was the same point I had made earlier. But I was too drunk to remember that. We lifted our glasses and failed to make contact for the toast. Somehow, we still managed to get the golden liquid down our throats.

I could see the light on upstairs as I stumbled up Dogwood Lane to my house. Maria had stayed awake waiting for me, which meant she was going to be mad. I resolved not to seem drunk, then spent about five minutes trying to get my house key into the lock. When I got inside, I forgot to be quiet and slammed the door shut behind me. After tossing my wool coat on the sofa, I tried to be stealthier climbing the stairs, but the wooden planks creaked in betrayal.

On the second-floor landing, I took a few seconds to gaze into the small bedroom we used for storage. Dust suffocated a cute teddy-bear rug that we'd bought impulsively long ago at a street festival. The room was meant to be a nursery, but that hadn't happened for us. We'd tried for about a year without success. Maria's OB/GYN couldn't find anything wrong with either of us, said we just needed to keep trying. Sex had stopped being fun, so we decided to go back on birth control for a while. It was only supposed to be a short break, but then I got the job working for Our Leader and, before we knew it, two years had passed. I knew Maria wanted to try again, but I had never gotten to a place where it felt like the right time.

With a deep breath—another attempt to sober up—

I took the next set of stairs up to the master bedroom. I opened the door a crack and peered inside.

Maria, who was watching me from the bed, asked, "You going to come in?"

I smelled strawberry. She had been vaping, a habit she knew I didn't like. The e-cigarettes often came out when she was mad at me.

"You didn't have to stay up," I said.

"You didn't have to stay so long at the bar."

"I know. I'm sorry. Scott—"

"I don't care about Scott."

I must have looked pathetic because Maria's anger seemed to melt at the sight of me. "I just," she began, "I just wanted one night to ourselves, without one of us checking our phones. It's not easy to turn off from my job, either, but I really tried tonight. I wanted you to try, too, Ham."

I loosened my tie. "Yeah. No, I get it. I do."

Maria switched off her Woozle e-book reader. "I really think it's a great idea," she said. "Starting your own PR firm, I mean."

I sat on the bed and put my hand on her leg. "I want to, but..."

My attention turned to a box on the floor. We hadn't opened it since moving to this house. There was never time. I wasn't sure what was in it. I was too tired to find out now.

I said, "I just don't think I can go out like *this*. You know?"

She raised her eyebrows. "Like what? You mean because of that intern? Blake, you want to quit. She wants you to leave. What's the problem?"

"I...I guess I just don't want her to think that she's won."

Maria surprised me with a kiss, just when I thought she was going to kick me out. "Oh God," she said with a laugh. "You taste like a cask. Tell me you ate something."

"I did, but to be honest, I probably should have had the Zand. Why'd you kiss me?"

She smiled. "You're a fighter, Blake. And stubborn. So am I. But we shouldn't stand around taking punches, either."

I agreed, but deep down I wasn't sure.

CHAPTER
FIVE

W HY DID IT always seem to be winter when I visited campus? From December through February, National University was a foreboding place to stroll, with cold wind whipping through spindly old trees and frozen clumps of brown leaf shards adding treachery to the black pavement walks.

Even with a bad leg, my walking partner didn't seem worried about slipping. Professor Althea Post was an old pro at navigating National University. The injury wasn't from a mere stumble, but in fact the result of a daring leap from a statue decades ago while escaping arrest. Al had been protesting the university's unfair treatment of the LGBTQ community. Five years later, the professor returned to Nat U to accept a teaching job, incidentally becoming the university's first transgender hire.

I'd taken Prof. Post's class in sophomore year and they had become sort of a mentor after that—academically, professionally, and in life generally. Al even helped me pick a diamond ring for Maria. The prof smartly informed me that my first choice was too dull for someone as vibrant as Maria Worthington. They redirected me to one containing rubies. Did Maria like it? Well, she agreed to marry my sorry butt, didn't she?

Al updated me on the latest dramas and politics at

Nat U, which ironically has theatre and political science as two of its most prominent majors. Woozle had again raised the prices of digital textbooks, this time by nearly 15 percent, the prof told me. The previous administration had abolished print textbooks as part of its "Lighten the Load" health-in-education initiative, for which Woozle had lobbied hard. The result was that no one could buy reduced price used books anymore. Althea said it was disproportionately affecting the lower-income students who had come to the school on scholarship.

"I can bring it up to Our Leader," I said. "He hasn't liked Woozle since before he was the President, when they didn't invite him to sing at Music Fest."

Althea shook their head. They didn't think much of Our Leader and didn't want his help. "Tell me, Blake: How many people did his mechanical beast *murder* before anyone at the Compound noticed it was missing?" asked the professor with the severe English accent of a mystery theater detective.

Although I had not divulged the classified, true reason for the previous day's PR subterfuge, I can't say I was surprised my former prof had deduced the truth. After all, Al had been one of the nation's most famous activist journalists. They still had the knack for seeing right through would-be opaque governments.

"Off the record?" I asked.

"Of course."

"No comment."

The prof clucked. "You can't decline comment off the record, darling, lest you be feasted upon by the media."

I smiled. "You'd be surprised how much crap reporters will eat these days."

They groaned. "The new class is a rather docile lot. I'm doing my best to put some fight into them."

"Doesn't Batman say something like that?"

"The Dark Knight says criminals are 'a superstitious and cowardly lot,'" they reminded me. "You'd do well to remember that reporters are not criminals."

"Of course." I knew it, though I couldn't say for sure all my colleagues did.

I attempted another sip of my vile coffee, which I'd ordered black because I thought it would help with my hangover. I still had a headache from the previous night but had not been able to bring myself to reschedule with Al. Based on the ghost town–like atmosphere on campus late Saturday morning, it appeared many Nat U students shared my post-drunken plight. Or maybe it was just too cold for sensible folk to be outside.

"I don't know how you can work for him," the professor remarked, not for the first time.

"The work is challenging."

"A nice way to put it."

"How would you put it?"

"Have you read *1984*?" With a clearing of the throat, the professor declared: "What you're doing is *dystopia* PR."

I laughed. Sometimes, I suspected Althea belonged to a revolutionary book club, though I'd never tell anyone. I'd sooner report my parents.

I said, "You'll be happy to know I have been thinking about quitting."

The statement was received with raised eyebrows.

"No, I mean it this time," I continued. "I'm just starting to feel as though...I don't have enough time for anything. It's like I keep putting off doing what I really want to do."

"Which is?"

"Just, you know, have time for things."

"What things?"

I felt too embarrassed to say it out loud.

Althea smiled knowingly. "How does Maria feel about it?"

"She thinks I work too much. But she works just as much as I do."

Al nodded thoughtfully. "You've been in that big house for a while."

I grimaced, understanding that the comment about my home wasn't about the building. "I...don't think we're ready for, you know...children."

"When will you be ready?"

"When we have time."

"When will you have time?"

"When I quit."

"And when will you quit?"

"I don't know."

When we reached the main quad, Al sat on a cedar bench and motioned for me to join. They reached into their purse and, almost magically, procured a white paper bag. "Fritter?"

Based on their smile, my eyes must have lit up. "Please!"

"I never took the time to start a family," said the professor while I gobbled down the glazed blueberry pastry. "I had suitors of course. *Many* suitors."

"However," said I, mimicking her accent. "None were suitable."

"Quite," the professor replied without missing a beat. "No, no," Al continued after we had a good laugh, "it was me who was the wrong fit. You see, I made my career the priority. That got me very far professionally, yes, but lately I've been thinking...it would be nice to have grandchildren around."

"Grandchildren in a dystopia?"

"So then," Al said, "that's the problem."

"What?"

They put their hand on mine. "Children will save us from darkness, Blake."

A yellow frisbee whizzed by. A dude in a fleece quarter-zip dove, caught the disc in midair, and slid across the frosted quad on his knees. "Hell yeah!" he roared.

"Holy shit, what a catch!" screeched his buddy, who was wearing a camera cap, which was a kind of knit hat with a built-in, always-on camera. "Holy fucking shit!"

Dryly, the professor observed, "Some guidance, naturally, is required."

"They're going to catch pneumonia," I said.

"See, you sound like a parent already."

"I *hope* they catch pneumonia."

"Or perhaps not."

I told Al that I was thinking of starting my own PR shop and becoming a consultant. "Then I could choose my clients, represent different kinds of people. Good people. You know?"

That brought on another smile. "Utopia PR."

I laughed.

The prof handed me a napkin, which I used to wipe the crumbs off my face. "I'd rather you return to journalism, of course, but this idea at least sounds like an improvement."

"I don't think they'd *let* me return to journalism at this point. Working for Our Leader has a way of killing one's appearance of fairness and objectivity."

"Perhaps," replied my mentor. "Well then, I think it's a grand idea, Blake."

CHAPTER
SIX

I T HAD FELT good talking about going into business for myself—thinking of this crazy idea as an actually possible future. Even so, I knew that quitting my current job wouldn't be as easy as submitting a resignation letter. It also seemed a little cruel to leave Scott to deal with the never-ending crisis of Our Leader's presidency, especially right after his demotion to deputy. The job did pay the bills, and I had no way of knowing how successful I could be on my own.

My job working for Our Leader had fallen into my lap about two years before the last presidential election. Every politician and their college-dropout brother seemed to be announcing bids, providing more than enough material for the next couple months of my blog. I was trying to decide who to write about first when, out of nowhere, I got a call from a number my phone didn't recognize. Normally, I might let such a call go to voice mail, but the area code was local, piquing my curiosity.

"Am I speaking to the Hammer?" asked the mystery caller, a man with a voice like a car salesman.

"Uh, yes, this is Blake Hamner."

"Oh, cool, so you mean the *n* is actually silent?"

"Uh, yes."

"I was worried I'd screw that up. That's why I used your pseudoephedrine."

I think he meant *pseudonym*, but I didn't think it wise to correct someone before they identified themselves. Smart move, because that's when he introduced himself as Scott Jones, political whiz for the liberal party. I'd seen Scott on Triple N gloating over the then-President's incompetence, but I'd never met him before.

"Love your blog, Blake. Love it. You don't know how many of my clients you've helped me get off the hook. For years, people have been giving me all the credit—and let's be honest—boatloads of cash, but I couldn't have done it without you. So, thanks. Really. Thanks."

"Uh, you're welcome." I wasn't sure what to say. "Pay it forward, I guess?"

"Or," he said pointedly, "I could pay you back."

That got my attention. Scott told me he'd just joined the campaign of a "very special candidate" running for president and wanted to get my opinion on if the guy really had a chance. "So, let's grab some Joe and see where things go!"

We met for coffee, which turned into lunch, which turned into beers, which turned into dinner, which turned into whiskeys, which turned into one heck of a hangover. A day later, Scott called to formally offer me a job with the campaign.

Our Leader could not have been elected in any other election year, but the incumbent was our least popular president ever. I mean, he was *really* bad, and everybody knew it. A lot of people who had voted for him jumped ship within the first year. The stench got so foul, his own political party broke tradition and primaried him. The party nominated Jason Stonybrook, a conservative's conservative, by more than 75 percentage points.

I might have had more doubts about Our Leader's ability to, you know, lead, if not for Stonybrook fashioning himself into something of a handmaid's nightmare. He ran on a platform that emphasized the sanctity of marriage, which is another way of saying he didn't want gay people to get married, which is another way of saying that they don't belong in our country. Not only did he want to take away their marriage licenses, but he wanted to make any homosexual public display of affection a crime. One of Stonybrook's actual rallying cries at campaign events was "Not in front of our children!" If he was displaying that much crazy on the campaign trail, one had to wonder what he would do if he had any power. Heterosexuals also could have found a lot of trouble under a Stonybrook administration, considering one of his campaign promises was to enforce abstinence before marriage. How would that have worked? Pants camera?

I told Scott during our epic first meeting that it would be no easy task selling Our Leader as the next president. Even though Stonybrook was a psychopath, he had the presidential look: broad smile, piercing eyes, baritone voice, hot doctor wife, three whip-smart kids, plus one cute poodle. He was a seasoned politician who ironically had a reputation of disagreeing with seasoned politicians, and he got bonus points for his fluency in economics and knowing which countries to bomb. All of that, coming after a president with the brain of a goldfish, made Stonybrook look pretty good. The only real question was whether the previous president's stink would carry to anyone from the same party.

Our candidate didn't have a lot of what I'd have called traditional assets for someone seeking our nation's highest office. He was too young, and he wasn't even good-looking. He didn't have or even want kids, let alone a wife. His name, Ernest Prawnmeijer, was hard to spell and intimidating to pronounce on the first try. Even when said correctly (Prawn-my-er), it sounded like a fishy hot dog. All that might be excusable if he had any political experience, but this guy didn't even have a business background.

Prawnmeijer did have one thing going for him: the guy could sing. His claim to fame was a TV singing competition where, with a steady tenor, he blew all the other contestants off the stage. The guy's voice was like syrup—not that fake corn-syrup crap; I mean this was 100 percent natural, Grade-A maple syrup. A record company had snapped him up like a hotcake, bequeathing him the much cooler pseudonym of "Our Leader." He'd owned the charts for five years, releasing three platinum records.

Our Leader's political career whirred into motion when a stoned radio DJ asked if he had any aspirations to be, like, you know, *our leader*.

"In fact, I do," Prawnmeijer had replied, cold as a cocktail shrimp.

The exchange got some laughs. But the singer had sounded serious and Scott said it got him thinking. The conservatives had flogged the liberal party in several consecutive elections, and most of the remaining liberal political stars were too old to run. Scott saw Our Leader as a fresh candidate who'd come into the race with a rabid following of young voters.

I didn't think I would, but I took the job. I guess I was getting tired of the measly pay I made with the blog. Maria never said she minded making so much more money than me, but I thought I could balance the scales a little. Here was my chance finally to hit the big time.

Scott and I positioned Our Leader as the ultimate underdog chasing the dream. Prawnmeijer, who we decided thenceforth to never call by his real name, was that guy who never got the girl, but who everyone rooted for because he sure could sing! Could Jason Stonybrook sing? No way. Jason Stonybrook was that asshole jock who picked on shrimps like Prawnmeijer. Well, high school was over and now it was Our Leader's time to shine.

Our Leader annihilated his political rival in the election. So much so, that Stonybrook basically disappeared afterward. As for Prawnmeijer, the knockout victory boosted his confidence to unparalleled levels. He started thinking of himself as invincible. He could do whatever he wanted, and nobody would stop him—or if they tried, they wouldn't be able to stop him. The more time Our Leader spent in the Compound, the less willing he was to take advice. It got increasingly difficult for all of us to do our jobs.

In retrospect, maybe Scott and I should have spent a little more time considering Our Leader's fitness for office before we got so carried away making him the most powerful man in the world.

CHAPTER
SEVEN

I MADE MY Monday morning coffee with enough cream and sugar to turn it caramel. That sweet, milky caffeine must have put me in a pretty good mood, because by the time my government limo arrived to pick me up from home, I'd decided to give Victoria a chance as our new boss.

I had the hover car to myself this time—even the driver was AI. So there was a lot of time to think this over. For one thing, having a little fresh blood leading the Comms department didn't seem like a completely bad idea. Scott was a good guy, but he *did* seem pretty burnt out, and he *was* kind of an alcoholic. And I guess that because I had always felt I was the logical successor to Scott as Comms Director, Victoria's selection in a way gave me an out whenever I was ready to move forward with my own public relations business, the one Althea had dubbed *Utopia PR*.

The Compound's security staff gave me no problems, but I started at the sight of the hound observing me from the green. The dog sat obediently at the foot of a marble statue that falsely depicted Our Leader as a military hero. Sunlight glanced off the so-called Hero Pup's golden tag. Its bright eyes cut through me like lasers.

When the hound stood, I took off at a jog toward the

main building. It was a long way and the weather was mild, so I was breathing heavily by the time I got inside. I went into the bathroom and splashed my face with cold water. When I removed my heavy winter coat, I discovered dark, wet circles emanating from the armpits of my buttoned gray shirt. I grabbed a handful of paper towels and stuck them inside to absorb the sweat.

"Can someone...please get me...an iced coffee?" I stammered as I opened the door to the Comms Situation Room. "With...cream and...sugar...please..."

Victoria wrinkled her nose and scowled at me. "I didn't know we had a swimming pool," she commented.

"Oh sure," said Scott. "You've never been? It's great. It's never crowded when I go, but then again, I'm usually there well past midnight."

"Shut up, idiot," she snapped.

I slicked back my hair to squeeze out the sweat, but the motion caused the paper towels in my shirt to fall to my belly, filling out the lower region of my shirt.

"Jesus, Blake," quipped Scott, "I think you might be getting fatter before our very eyes."

I pulled my shirt from my belt to free the towels. Victoria skittered back as the moist paper balls rolled across the floor.

Apologizing, I gathered up the rags and tossed them into the garbage can. I staggered toward one of the webbed chairs and lowered myself inside. "Can I just...can I just rest here...for a minute? And if you...don't mind...iced coffee...please."

Victoria groaned like an inconvenienced teenager. She tapped the intercom on the conference table and said, "Can someone bring in a pitcher of water and some glasses?" She looked at me. "Better make it three pitchers."

"You'll have to drink fast," said Scott, frowning. "We're not going to be able to stay long."

I turned to my new boss for an explanation and she positively beamed. "That's right, I thought you boys could use some fresh air, so I'm sending you on a field trip."

I gritted my teeth. "Field trip?"

"I need you to check how Project Milkman is progressing."

Oh no, I thought. *Not Project Milkman.*

People in power tend to suffer from one kind of mania or another. The job of a PR rep is to keep the powerful person from showing it. To keep the job, however, the successful flack mustn't say no to everything. If I always told Our Leader no, he would quickly replace me with someone who'd say yes. To be clear, I wasn't worried about my job; I was worried about humankind.

There were two schools of thought on how to decide which of my psychopathic boss's crazy ideas to allow. A lot of PR reps would say yes to the least insane concept—the one that's eccentric, maybe even a little worrisome, but at worst results in a containable amount of damage. Although I respect that strategy, Scott and I took a different approach with Our Leader. What we'd do is allow the mad ideas that sounded most unlikely to work. We'd tell him, *We can do that thing, sure! But let's do a soft launch and not tell the public about it until we're sure it's ready.* Our Leader would get to do his crazy project, and when it inevitably failed, that was no problem because the public never knew about it in the first place. Besides, by the time testing was done, Our Leader had usually forgotten the idea and moved on to something else.

Project Milkman was one of these insane ideas I knew would never come to anything. We were about six months into its imminent failure. Our Leader had wanted to come up with a way to keep his people "happy," which is to say submissive and non-questioning. At first, I thought he'd said he wanted an "opiate for the masses," à la that Karl Marx quote about religion. But it turned out that Our Leader had said *opioid.* He wanted to drug everyone into feeling good about his administration.

The plan was to bring back old-fashioned milk delivery, with the glass bottles and the guys in the white paper hats, but drug the milk so as to calm everyone down and discourage dissidence. Somewhat cleverly, the plan fulfilled a campaign promise to return our nation to the golden age.

OK, Project Milkman may sound pretty evil, but it's also pretty stupid. Soylent green isn't people—it's fiction. It's not easy to implement something like Milkman in real life, especially not the way Our Leader wanted. Even if we could deliver milk to everybody, we certainly couldn't force everybody to drink it. Some people are lactose intolerant, and other people just don't like the taste of milk. Also, there was no way to control the dosage because even bona fide milk drinkers consume different amounts. For example, Maria makes sure to drink three glasses a day, whereas I get most of my Vitamin D from creamer. Wouldn't a person who doesn't drink milk, or someone like me who barely drinks any, figure out fast that all their dairy-loving friends were turning into cattle?

So yes, we let Our Leader have that crazy concept, but only as a pilot project, which in government is never a serious thing. We convened a few scientists to test out the milk on a few trial communities that voted for Jason Stonybrook in the election. They were to come back to us in one year with a report on the project's feasibility, which we may or may not show to Our Leader, depending on whether he ever brought it up again.

In the elevator, Scott slapped me on the back. His hand made a squishing sound and he had to wipe off my sweat on his suit pants.

"Maybe next time don't run," he commented.

I eyed him suspiciously. "How did you know I ran?"

Scott took a gulp from his yellow sports drink, which advertised itself as *Athletes' #1 Choice for Supercharged Performance.* Apparently, it was also the top choice of overweight, middle-aged men. "We saw you on the monitor," Scott said. "What was that about?"

"The hound," I said gravely. "After what happened yesterday...I don't know. I just don't trust it."

Before Scott could respond, the door opened, and a cold gust of wind blew into the elevator. Shielding my eyes from the sun, I strode out onto the roof toward a hornet-shaped ship floating about a foot off the ground. It looked like the old helicopters of my childhood, but without the big spinning blades on top. Advances in hover technology had rendered the noisy rotors unnecessary, so the big black machine flew almost silently. Pretty dang eerie.

I was a little surprised to see the vehicle ready to fly. Apparently, Victoria couldn't wait to get rid of us and had already briefed the pilot.

The cabin door was closed, and the pilot didn't seem to see us approach. He was chewing on a sub—possibly meatball, based on the tomato sauce smeared across his cheek. I waved frantically at the door to get his attention, but the guy was too absorbed in the sandwich and the thrashing rock music he had on his radio. Finally, I went around front and jumped up and down in front of the windshield. Looking a little annoyed, the pilot pressed a button and waved me back around.

Scott and I climbed inside the private passenger cabin. "Don't stand in front of the choppah," the pilot wheedled through an intercom that lent a robotic buzz to his voice. "It's dangerous to stand in front of the choppah."

"Maybe if you hadn't been wrapping your mouth around those saucy balls, I wouldn't have had to," I called back.

Scott snickered. "Saucy balls. That's my Hammer."

"Someone's wicked grumpy today," sneered the pilot, but he put down the sub and took the controls.

Because flying in these things always made me a little nervous, I turned to Scott for a little small talk. "So, any idea what happened to Rico?"

"Oh shit, I forgot to ask this morning. I was going to. He's probably fine."

We left it at that.

The Compound shrank into a miniature below our

flying chariot. The bird's-eye view made the beige base look even uglier.

CHAPTER
EIGHT

O UR STEEL CHARIOT transported us deep into a
snow-covered country. Just as the regal buildings
of Washington felt like a distant memory, we descended
into a vast farm. The white frosting lent some real charm
to the dairy operation, belying its true nature as a drug
lab. I started to make a note in my journal that this whole-
some image was something we could advertise, but I
stopped when I remembered that Project Milkman
should never get that far.

The hovercraft landed in a large paved area that looked
out of place in such rural environs. The great lot held
a fleet of milk trucks with actual wheels, a rare sight in
this new age of hover vehicles. Each light-blue vehicle
featured a cartoon cow, standing on her hind legs, and
sipping on a glass of what I could only presume was her
own milk through a fun straw.

I was feeling a little sick from the flight and popped
out the door as soon as the pilot said it was safe. A man
in a white lab coat came out to greet us. He clapped my
back and I nearly lost my breakfast.

"Boys! Boys! It's good to see you again!"

This was the project's lead scientist, Dr. Norbert Falz.
He was a wiry old man in his seventies with bushy gray
hair around his mouth and sticking out of his ears. He

was known for publishing a groundbreaking study on climate change that, while agreeing it was a real and imminent threat, declared that there was nothing anybody could do about it, so we might as well have a grand old time. The previous administration, composed of conservative businessmen who had long sought to do nothing on environmental issues but could never come up with a good reason why not, embraced the Falz findings.

Our Leader was of course a liberal, so one of his first presidential acts was to make a big show of throwing out the Falz study. We still hadn't gotten around to saving the planet, but we had at least gotten the ball rolling by ordering a new study from better scientists.

When I started looking for a quack to head up Project Milkman, I found Dr. Falz haunting the halls of the Environmental Protection Agency, presumably looking for something to do. Since we didn't want him anywhere near global warming, we put him in charge of Project Milkman.

"What brings you here?" asked Falz.

"Just wanted to see how things are going," I said.

"Excellent!"

Scott furrowed his giant brow. "Really?"

"What?" asked the scientist.

"The pilot projects are...excellent?"

Falz laughed. "Oh no, of course not. I was just saying that I'm glad you've come."

I took a deep breath. "And the pilots?"

The doctor furrowed his brow. "The who?"

I answered through gritted teeth. "The trial communities. How are they doing?"

"Oh! There is promise, maybe." He paused. "But perhaps it would be best if I showed you in person."

Scott had out his notebook. "Before we go, could you go over the production and delivery system?"

"Why, certainly," said Falz.

This is where I phased out for a while. I just couldn't get over how pointless it was sending Scott and me here. The only thing that made sense was that Victoria didn't want us to get in her way on her first day as Communications Director. I supposed that she had a plan to impress Our Leader, or more likely, to dirty our reputations.

I checked my phone to see if she'd made any moves yet, but I didn't find anything. Triple N Online's most-clicked news story was a profile on the hound. Being a machine, the hound didn't have much of a backstory, but apparently several readers had written in to supply possible origins for the Hero Pup. One involved the soul of a heroic fire dog who died while saving an old woman trapped on the forty-sixth floor of a burning apartment building. The story went that that the pooch's spirit entered the hound, imbuing valorous tendencies into its steel skull. At the end of the article, there was a link to our naming contest.

It appeared that my spin was working even better than anticipated, which made me even angrier that my job could be in danger.

Scott nudged me. "Ready for the tour, Blake?"

"Huh?" I looked up from my device and absorbed the kooky gaze of Dr. Falz. "Yeah, let's go."

The farm was located at nearly equal distance from the trial villages of Rose Bay, Avalon, and Chesterville. We drove first to Rose Bay in one of the milk trucks. It seemed like a fun way to travel until I realized there was no backseat and the three of us would have to squeeze together in the front, which had a long, cushioned bench stretching from one side to the other. Dr. Falz took the driver's seat, and Scott and I played Rock-Paper-Scissors for the window. I won, naturally, so that loser had to squeeze between the doc and me.

Getting on the move revealed the big downside to vehicles with actual wheels—we felt every bump and pothole on the rural country road. Scott's voice vibrated in tremolo, "Fu-u-u-u-uck thi-i-i-is ri-i-i-ide."

It took me a while to understand what we saw in Rose Bay. Everything looked normal. We drove down Main Street in a trickling stream of cars. A young couple kissed outside a cafe. An old lady stepped out of a bank counting twenty-dollar bills. A child, maybe six or seven, chased his older brother up the sidewalk, his mom yelling after them not to cross the street.

The normalcy of the situation worried me immensely. If the drug was working without noticeable side effects, that would mean Project Milkman was a huge success.

"I'm getting out for a second," I said, opening the door as we came to a stop at a red light. "I need to check something."

Dr. Falz looked confused. "There's no need to—"

But I was gone. I went straight for the dive bar and stepped inside. It wasn't a drink I needed, but honest folks. I sat down at the counter and ordered a beer so that I wouldn't look suspicious. Anyway, they had my favorite IPA.

I leaned over to the middle-aged man watching Triple N and asked, "Any news?"

He grunted. "Just the fucking same."

The profanity took me aback. Impressive that the scientists could fashion a calming drug that still allowed people to speak colorfully.

"Our Leader is a fucking moron!" he continued. "And the news just lets him be one!"

A woman farther down the counter chimed in: "He's not *my* leader! I voted for Jason Stonybrook!"

"Heh," I said, and took a long sip of beer. Now I understood.

Scott burst inside, with the doc close behind him. "What the hell are you doing, Blake?"

"The drug doesn't work," I declared. "Everyone here is exactly the same."

"Of course they're the same," said Dr. Falz. "Like I said before we left, no one in Rose Bay is drinking our milk. This is our *control* group."

With a sigh, I deserted my half-finished beer and followed my government colleagues out the door. Returning to the milk truck, I asked Scott if he would take the middle seat again. He impolitely declined.

It was a quick ride into Avalon; the only traffic was parked on the side of the street.

"Sleepy town," commented Scott.

"Where is everyone?" I asked.

"Sleeping," answered Dr. Falz.

I checked my watch. "But it's almost noon!"

"True, true," he replied glumly. Falz eventually found a space to park the van and we got out to take a closer look. All the shops were closed, even though most of them displayed hours indicating they should be open. It was so quiet I could hear the electric utility wires humming overhead.

"You might say the milk did its job too well," the doctor said.

We walked a little more, turning off the main drag into a residential street. I saw a tricycle on its side on one person's lawn, but there were no children anywhere.

I shuddered. "I have to admit this is freaking me out a little."

A loud creak spun me around on my toes. A teenage boy with a shovel staggered out from one of the houses and plunged face-first into the snow.

"But they're all just sleeping right?" I asked, suddenly filled with dread about the possible reaction if news about this town got out. "They're not—"

"Dead?" hooted Dr. Falz with a maniacal laugh. "No. Not yet, anyway. And we are planning to adjust the dosage, naturally. We think that might help."

"How long have they been like this?" asked Scott.

"About a week, but the effects should wear off soon."

"Well," said Scott, "I guess one positive thing is that everyone is taking the milk."

I turned to Falz. "Hey, that's right, how did you deal with people that don't like to drink milk, or the lactose intolerant?"

"Ah," said the doctor, stroking his beard. "We created many varieties of the milk, including skim, one percent, two percent, lactose-free, almond, and coconut. All of those come in chocolate or strawberry flavors. Delivering milk bottles to each house ensures everyone has access to the milk, and when the milkman returns to pick up empties, he confirms the effects and lets us know if anyone isn't consuming the opioid."

"Elixir," I offered.

"What?"

"Don't say opioid. That won't market well."

"Of course," said Falz. "Anyhoo, if someone isn't drinking the milk, we send over a soldier to offer a little 'encouragement.'" He put the last word in air quotes and raised his eyebrows suggestively.

Scott frowned. "Would that...would that scale?"

"To the whole country?" I answered. "Probably not."

"To be honest, we haven't had to take *that* step very often. What we discovered to be most effective was stamping a one-week expiration date on the container—it really increased people's urgency to drink at the pace we require."

As we walked back to the van, I thought I saw something on the roof of one of the homes. I shielded my face from the sun and peered up at the shingles, but I didn't see anything out of the ordinary.

"You all right, Hamner?" asked Scott.

"I...I don't know," I said. "I thought I saw someone up on the roof."

"Santa Claus, perhaps?" needled Falz, that asshole.

Scott laughed. "Last place someone should be on this kind of drug." Portraying a man with two fingers as legs,

Scott's left hand walked off an imaginary roof and took a dive into his right palm.

I didn't think Chesterville could be any worse than Avalon. However, when we cruised down our third Main Street in as many hours, we found it crowded with townsfolk who seemed immune to the cold weather. In unison, they turned to stare at our dairy vehicle. It wasn't a look of confusion, or even irritation. It was a look of pure thirst.

A man moaned, "Miiiilk..."

From a blue stroller, a baby dropped its bottle. The plastic container smacked the sidewalk and rolled into the street, empty.

"Chesterville at first seemed to be a great success," narrated Falz. "The drug did everything we wanted it to. But...we ran into a *slight* problem of supply and demand."

As a PR expert, I know BS when I hear it. "Are you saying that they're all addicted, and the withdrawal turns them into zombies?"

That's when the villagers charged.

"Close the window!" I cried to Scott.

Shaken into action, Scott tugged at the little electric window switch. A townie got a hand partway inside and squealed when the glass pinched her finger. Scott opened the window a centimeter to free the finger and then shut it the rest of the way.

The finger lady started slapping the window, and the other townies followed, pounding the side of the van and pleading for their drug.

"Milk!" demanded one zombie.

"Mo' milk!" cried a toddler.

A heavyset biker-type bellowed in a deep voice, "It's good for the bones!"

My partner fluttered his hands in a panic. "I don't get it! Why do they think *we* have milk?"

To which I shoved him in the arm and exclaimed, "We're sitting in a milk truck!"

That was about all I could take. There was no way to spin this disaster. "Falz," I said.

"Yes?" The wacko frothed with mirth. He actually seemed to be enjoying this.

"Get us the heck out of here!"

Falz stepped on the gas and we burst forth, narrowly missing a few women who managed to dive out of the way. The angry mob attempted to follow but gave up as we put a few blocks between us.

"Oh God," whimpered Scott. He was looking back at the crowd through the side mirror.

I couldn't see anything from where I was sitting. "What?"

"They're...I think they're turning on...on...each other..."

Mad old Dr. Falz wiped tears of joy from his eyes.

OK, so I might have exaggerated a little bit about what we saw in Chesterville. One thing I swear I didn't stretch was how much of a lunatic Falz was.

"Can we fire that doctor guy?" asked Scott when were back in the hovercraft and headed home. "I mean, that doctor guy is nuts, right? I'm not sure, but I think I saw him sucking milk from a baby bottle at one point. Like a baby goat!"

"A kid."

"No, I mean like a little goat!"

For a (former) Communications Director, Scott didn't have much of a vocabulary. But he did have a point about the mad doctor. Leaning back in my black leather seat, I said, "I think we need to do more than fire Falz. I think we need to shut down Project Milkman immediately."

Scott agreed. "No good PR can come from that crazy bat shit."

"Guano."

"What?"

"A bat's... number two...is called guano," I explained.

"Honestly, I don't see how that's any less offensive than shit," said Scott, wrinkling his nose in disgust. He flipped through his notes. "Anyway, I don't know. Our Leader seemed pretty psyched about Project Milkman working out. You know he still hasn't gotten over the fact that some people didn't vote for him."

"That was almost two years ago. He brought it up again?"

"Last week at Christmas dinner. I mean, the Annual Late-December Holiday Celebration."

My stomach rumbled. The pilot appeared to be eating something. Another hoagie? Or was it the same hoagie as before? No, it definitely was a new hoagie. Should have asked him to pick up a few more.

"Where did he even get that—" my colleague and I spoke in unison.

"—baby bottle?" Scott finished.

"—hoagie?" I said.

I noticed a lunch box sandwiched between Scott's feet. Salivating, I asked, "What've you got in there?"

"Oh, Victoria asked me to bring back a few samples of the milk."

"Samples?" I was about to ask for more information when the hovercraft jolted sharply to the right. There was an explosion of white as my head smacked against the wall, but I managed to maintain consciousness.

Scott put a hand on my shoulder. "You all right, Blake? I don't think you're bleeding."

I said I was OK, though really it hurt like heck.

He stretched out from his seatbelt to reach for his notebook, which had fallen on the floor, then screamed into the mic on his headset. "You trying to kill us?"

"Sah-ree, boys," replied the pilot. "There was a flying man." He said it as if it happened all the time. "Came wicked close to spraying his guts all over the windshield like a mosquito."

"A *flying* man?" Scott repeated incredulously.

"Looked like a knight, but without the horse, you know?"

I wondered if there were magic mushrooms in our pilot's sub. The idea of engaging in his delusions amplified the pounding in my cranium, so I clicked off the radio and shut my eyes.

CHAPTER
NINE

OUR RETURN TO the Compound's bright white hallways intensified my headache. I also felt incredibly tired; I'd fallen asleep up in the sky, but the nap had only served to make me groggy.

Scott huffed when we got to his office. Someone had removed his nameplate from the door and replaced it with one for *Victoria Chu*.

"I knew she was going to take the office," moaned Scott, "but I just thought I'd have a little more time to gather my things."

I shifted the lunch box in my arms. "Well, we do need to give her these milk samples. This *is* kind of a time-saver, if you think about it."

My friend tried to glare away my tightly pursed smile—in vain. He turned his anger to the doorknob, wrenching the thing open and bursting inside dramatically.

"You could have knocked," said Victoria with a yawn. She was reclining in Scott's great big leather office chair.

"Couldn't you have taken Rico's office?" demanded Scott.

She shook her head. "I like the view of the Rose Garden."

"Is this a new desk?" I asked the question because it was a light pine and I was sure Scott's was coffee brown.

"No," she replied, pointing to a bottle of Pine-Sol on the windowsill. "I just cleaned it."

"Hashtag #MenAreGross," commented Debbie, who was hunched over her phone in a corner by the window. She'd been so still, I hadn't seen her when I came in.

I shot Scott a look of disgust—I'd had lunch with him in here many times and eaten off that desk when it was coffee brown—but he was too busy seething to care what I thought about his hygiene.

"Would you please get off the Commander?" Scott yelled.

Victoria's eyes widened. "Excuse me?"

"The Commander only gets to hold one ass, and it ain't yours, Vicky."

"What?!"

"The 'Commander' is what Scott calls the chair," I explained, somewhat apologetically. The milk samples in my arms were starting to get heavy, and frankly I didn't have time for this nonsense, so I plopped the lunch box down on a nearby table.

The heavy *thunk* got our boss's attention. "Is this the–?" she asked.

"It does the body good," I replied with a showman's grin. "Well, actually...no, maybe not in this case."

Victoria groaned. "Don't tell me. Put it in a report and have it on my desk before you leave."

Scott gasped. "Today?"

"Is that going to be a problem?"

I tried to stay calm. "It's been kind of a long day, and

it's already five. Couldn't we do it first thing tomorrow morning?"

Victoria shook her head with disappointment. "See, boys, this is exactly the reason why I get this office. You can take twenty minutes to move Scott into his new arrangement, then get to work. When you have the report done, you can leave. Sound good?"

"Where," stammered Scott, "where is my...new arrangement?"

"Take the elevator down to Sub-Basement Level 3," Victoria replied brightly. "Someone down there can help you."

"Sub... Sub... Sub-Basement...Level 3?"

He had good reason to be flustered. Considering that you had to go down ten basement floors just to get to the first sub-basement level, descending to SB-3 was like taking an elevator to the thirteenth floor of an upside-down office building.

Scott pleaded, "Wait, can't I just have Rico's office?"

"No, that's reserved for the Press Secretary. You're Deputy Communications Director, and we don't have an office up here for that role."

"But there currently is no Press Secretary!"

"Currently," she agreed.

"But..."

I picked up one of the boxes with Scott's stuff that Victoria had packed up unceremoniously and led him out of the office before he could make any more trouble. I was furious about having to work late. Victoria hadn't even bothered to thank us for making the trip!

"Wait," she called after us.

Could I have been too rash? Was Victoria going to be a semi-decent boss, after all?

She had the lunch box in her hands, and before I could say anything, she dropped it into the top of my carton. I grunted as my arms sank with the added weight.

"Would you mind delivering these samples to the lab on your way down? I'll let the hacks know you're coming. Thanks!"

She slammed the door as we walked out.

The milk sloshed about in the containers as our elevator rattled its way down into the recesses of the Compound. The wet sound made me nauseous, and I felt much relief when we finally dropped off the milk samples with the science geeks on Basement Level 2. Returning to the stainless-steel box, Scott hesitated to press the DOWN button.

"At least there *is* an elevator," I said in a futile effort to cheer the man up.

This wasn't a frivolous point. The first architectural plans for the Compound had included only a steep set of spiral stairs. Whether this was an omission or calculated evil, I don't know. Luckily, we noticed it before it was too late. A bunch of high-ranking government staff, including yours truly, made a fuss and we got our elevator. The compromise, apparently, was that they bought the cheapest one they could find.

Scott moaned as I summoned the elevator. When the doors opened, I had to push him inside.

The thing took a while to get to Sub-Basement Level

3. It seemed like the distance between sub-basement levels was twice as long as that between the higher floors. Finally, the doors opened into a stale office space with puke-brown cubicles as far as the eye could see. SB-3 was home to the Messaging Department, essentially the grunts who handled all the low-level and miscellaneous communications, like Our Leader posters, subliminal radio ads, and patriotic product placement in popular TV shows.

"How would you pitch this?" I asked Scott.

"Pitch what?"

"This floor. It's a game Maria and I play sometimes."

Scott blinked.

"For example, I might say, 'Behold the brilliance of fluorescent light in Sub-Basement Level 3! Who needs windows?'"

"This isn't helping."

We approached a bored receptionist sipping herbal tea. Scott was too busy scowling, so I spoke up for him. "Hi, Tanya," I said, reading her name from a dusty stack of business cards. "This is Scott Jones. We were told there's a desk for him somewhere on this level?"

Without a word, Tanya turned to her monitor and began clicking around. It wasn't completely clear if she was helping or ignoring us, so after a minute I asked if she'd found him.

"Mm-hm," she answered, standing up with her eyes still trained on the monitor. "Follow me."

We followed the receptionist to a cubicle positioned nearly in the center of the grand maze. It contained a worn fabric chair, a gray plastic desk, and a PC that looked over a decade old. Some of the letters had rubbed off the computer's keyboard, which was full of food crumbs and human hair.

"How am I ever going to find my desk every day?" Scott whimpered as he dropped his box on the floor.

"Welcome to Hell," greeted the man in the cubicle across from Scott's. A bush of chest hair burst disgustingly from the man's shirt collar. The gremlin swiveled back to his computer screen before we could respond.

"So, um," I said to Scott to change the subject. "How about you write up what we saw at the milk facility and Avalon? I'll take Rose Bay and Chesterville."

Scott nodded glumly and sat down. The dinky chair squeaked.

"Hey, we're going to get your office back," I said. "Victoria may have won this round, but she doesn't have your experience. It's just a matter of time before she stumbles, and then you'll be back on top of the Commander."

"It's just..." He let out a deep sigh. "I miss the way he held my butt."

I felt bad. "You want to share my office? It's pretty big, and we could steal a chair from the Comms Situation Room."

Blake managed a smile. "Thanks, Blake, but no. I can't do that to you. I'll earn my way back upstairs, just like you said. We'll beat Victoria, fair and square."

When I got wireless service back on the ground level, I texted Maria to tell her I would be home late and not to wait up for dinner. She said that was OK—her bosses wanted her to stay for a late meeting to talk about the direction of her show, anyway. She added a vomiting emoji.

My stomach rumbled. I knew I wouldn't be able to write a report on Project Milkman without eating something. Our Leader had a personal chef who could make meals on request twenty-four hours a day, seven days a week—but only Our Leader could ask, and the President wasn't big on favors. Anyway, I didn't want to bother him. We also had a cafeteria, but it was only open for breakfast and lunch due to budget cuts. So, it would have to be a snack-machine supper tonight.

My phone beeped. Maria again. She'd written: *Don't eat snacks for dinner again.*

My wife knew me all too well. I responded with a non-committal thumbs-up.

I peered hopelessly through the glass of the vending system. Should have asked that pilot to get me a sub! The only thing in there that could possibly fill me up would be the least satisfying—CM-2, a miniature tube containing two capsules. The label read: *A Complete Meal in 2 Pills!*

I'd had a bad experience with CM-2 the first and only time I'd tried it. Per the directions, I had swallowed two pills with a glass of water, but because they didn't taste like anything, I hadn't felt like I'd really eaten. So, I'd had a couple more with a shot of bourbon—you know, for flavor. When I still didn't feel satisfied, I had bought a bag of chips and drank more bourbon.

What happened next haunts me to this day.

Just seeing that green tube again made me gag. I couldn't bring myself to buy it a second time. I decided to instead make a meal out of honey buns, nut bars, and cheese curls. Sorry, Maria.

I brought the snacks to my office and spread the fatty mess across my wooden desk. I spent most of my time in the Comms Situation Room, but in fact, I had a pretty nice space of my own on the ground level. It wasn't big but I'd personalized the space with baseball bobbleheads and a framed, autographed poster of my favorite late-night TV host, Funnyman Dan. It was from about a year ago when Maria had surprised me on my birthday with tickets to a live taping of *Nobody Likes to Stay Up This Late with Funnyman Dan*. I'd laughed my head off.

My window looked out at the Rose Garden. It had gotten dark, so I couldn't see much now. Squinting through my reflection in the glass, I thought I saw two violet lights floating in the air, approximately two feet off the ground. My heart pulsed. The hound?

I shut the blinds and shivered deeply. Hoping to retake control of my emotions, I focused my attention on the white digital picture frame on my desk. The ever-cycling slide show was in the thick of our wedding photos. I made up a caption for the current image: *Wearing a white dress and looking just as stunningly beautiful as she does today, Maria Worthington shoves delicious wedding cake into the mouth of the young-and-slim Blake Hamner. Unwittingly, Maria has pushed her trim groom down an ignoble path of gluttony that is sure to haunt her in Blake's increasingly doughy years to come.*

I popped open the cheese curls and got to work on my report.

CHAPTER
TEN

I GOT HOME a little after eight thirty, feeling completely exhausted from the day's travels. My wife barely looked up from the TV as I walked in. She had on some kind of boating show and was holding a glass of pinot noir.

She pointed to the bottle on the coffee table. "You better take some before I finish it."

My wife sounded pissed off, but I was pretty sure it had nothing to do with me.

"What are you watching?"

"*Splash-Q with Johnny Blue*. My new bosses say it's the future of news."

I looked back at the TV. *"This?"*

"This."

I sat next to her on the sofa and poured myself a glass of red.

Ever see a dolphin show at an aquarium, where the audience sits in big bleachers in front of a tank and watches divers toss fish into the water to make the mammals do tricks? *Splash-Q* was kind of like that, except there was a reporter zigzagging around the tank in a speed boat. Someone in the audience would raise their hand and he'd speed over to take their question. Sometimes they'd get splashed and the crowd would laugh.

Johnny Blue's latest victim was a skinny, tan woman in a thin white T-shirt and—very obviously—no bra. "Sorry about that!" cracked the host, who had clearly meant to do it. "Maybe I can make it up to you...over dinner?"

The woman blushed amid uproarious laughter from the audience.

"Screw this show," commented Maria.

Blue grinned. "Hope I didn't overstep..."

"Oh, I don't mind," the questioner cooed. "Lucky for you...I don't mind getting a little *wet*."

A howl from the bleachers.

"Screw this show," my wife said again.

"Ooh la la," replied Johnny with a little growl. "OK, girl, what's your question?"

"My question is just, like, I guess, why do we have to have so many foreigners in our country?"

"Ooh, tough one," he replied.

"So now what?" I asked Maria. "Is he going to take that one himself?"

She gritted her teeth. "Just watch."

The host pointed into the air, and the camera panned up to reveal a figure in a harness and hanging from a large white crane over the great pool. I was astonished to see it was Senator Gabby Choi! Actually, it wasn't a complete surprise; she was up for reelection.

"Senator!" the host called. "Do you have an answer for the pretty young lady?"

Choi gave a passionate response about the importance of immigration to the fabric of our country, and how she herself had come from a family of immigrants.

The host cut her off with a big, showy yawn. It got

a big laugh from the crowd. "Folks, do we like that answer?"

"No!" the crowd called back.

He smiled. "In that case, do you know what time it is?"

"Splash time!" they cheered.

That's when Senator Gabby Choi got *dunked*.

Maria changed the channel and screamed with agitation.

"Honey," I said, kissing her cheek, "why were you watching that?"

She shook her head. "You know that meeting I had to stay late for? It was about finding a 'new direction' for my show. Apparently, Joe Steele and the other bigwigs at Woozle think Triple N is getting too old fashioned. They asked if I'd seen *Splash-Q* yet. They said it was getting really good ratings."

I motioned to the TV. *"That?"*

"That. Apparently, Joe Steele is a horny little nerd." Maria tipped back her glass and drained it.

"You're a better reporter than that moron in the boat," I said.

"Am I? All I do is read the text they put in front of me. I'm a news reader."

"You're more than that," I said.

It was almost violent, the way she shrugged her arms. "A news reader who adds a pop of *color*, then. But that's the whole reason they should keep my show on the air, right? What I do appeals to a wider audience! This shit? This shit appeals to rich frat boys on spring break!"

My wife's language irked me, but I held back making a point of it. Instead, I just said, "Someone there must agree with you."

"Oh yeah?" she snapped. "I would sure love to meet them."

We'd had talks like this before, and it was hard to know what to say. She was probably right, but was it better for me to agree with her or try to cheer her up by saying it wasn't so?

I ended up going with an old PR tactic—changing the subject.

"My day sucked, too. I really was going to give Victoria a chance, but she's even worse than I thought."

"What happened?"

"Well, I can't really go into a lot of details." This was one of the problems with working for Our Leader but being married to a journalist—most of my day was classified. "Long story short, she made Scott and me go on a stupid trip, moved Scott's stuff out of his old office before he even had a chance to process his demotion, then made us stay late to write a report about the stupid trip."

"That does sound stupid," she said tiredly. "So, what do you want to do?"

An Our Leader spot came on the television. He was jogging around the suburbs, singing a hit single from ten years ago that had become an anthem for his government. "We live in a beautiful land! Don't mess with our beautiful land! I'll keep you safe if you take my hand!"

He wasn't really jogging. Scott had brought in a special-effects guy to stick Our Leader's head on a stunt double.

"Blake?"

"Oh, I don't know what I should do," I said morosely.

"I meant tonight. What do you want to do tonight?"

"Oh," I said, checking my watch. "It's pretty late.

Maybe just read books in bed? Honestly, I could go right to sleep."

Maria looked disappointed. "I was thinking maybe we could, you know, start trying again?"

"Oh, uh..."

My wife is sexy as all heck, and I love her so much, but I just couldn't that night. I was still feeling so tired and annoyed, I think. I tried to explain that to her, and she said she understood, but I could tell that I'd upset her.

CHAPTER
ELEVEN

I GOT SWEET revenge on Victoria the next morning by working remotely from the diner with my favorite colleagues, Joe Coffee and Julie Donut. OK, so I ordered two jellies, but at least I asked Sarah to send them out separately and to wait a few minutes before bringing me the second.

"That's not how diets work, you know," Sarah commented, wiping the counter with a cream-colored rag.

"Who said I was on a diet?"

"Your wife," she said, reaching into a glass case to retrieve my first pastry. "I suppose if you do lose weight, you should think about trademarking your one-donut-at-a-time approach. You could call it the 'Sequential Donut Diet.' Could make a lot of money!"

Scowling, I teased, "I didn't know you moonlighted as a comedian."

She walked away laughing. "OK, hon, I'll be back soon with your second donut. Sounds like you might need it."

Maria didn't seem to mind my choice of breakfast, possibly because she couldn't actually see it. My wife, the news anchor, was smiling magnanimously from the diner's television. She was skillfully managing a contentious debate between a veterinarian and a grey-hound's racing manager. There was something hypnotic about the segment, and I polished off the donut quicker than anticipated. As I was licking the sugar from my fingers, *BREAKING NEWS* burst onto the screen.

"This just in," Maria announced. "A leaked video of a secret government experiment in the towns of Rose Bay, Avalon, and Chesterville!"

Some strawberry jam dribbled out of my mouth. Seconds later, my phone started blowing up with panicked messages from Scott:

Come back

Now

Duck!

I must admit that last message gave me a real scare. I was about to take cover when I realized that Scott's auto-correct might again be to blame. I almost blurted out the curse he had meant to write, but thankfully held it inside.

Up on the screen, a greatly alarmed Maria continued. "The government appears to be testing a drug delivered secretly to the towns' residents through...through...bottles of milk?" She was reading from the teleprompter, and it was clear she was learning the details at the same time as the viewers. "Wow. Through bottles of *milk*. Some speculate that the drug may be meant to suppress any ill will toward Our Leader."

Sarah was holding some half-and-half and I saw her grip tighten around the carton. Perhaps remembering who it was I worked for, the restaurateur looked at me in a rage, and I got a bad feeling that I wasn't going to get that second donut after all.

# #

The PR team stood agape at the TV in the Comms Situation Room. Triple N had somehow gotten footage of the zombie Chestervillians who had surrounded our milk truck.

I was debating whether it should be *Chester-vill-i-ans* or *Chester-vill-ains* when Our Leader burst into the room shouting, "Fake news!"

"In high definition," I murmured to Scott, as Prawnmeijer continued to rant in the background. We'd learned how to turn the President's profanity into white noise during moments of crisis.

"Did you see any reporters?" interrogated Victoria. "Photographers on the roofs?"

"Just Spider-Man," I retorted sarcastically, but the question did get me thinking about the weird feeling I'd gotten in Avalon, the sleepy town. Something had made me look up to the rooftops, but I hadn't seen anybody.

Scott offered a hearty guffaw, but he was late to the punch as usual. "Oh, because Spider-Man's secret identity is a photographer! Good one, Blake. But wait, Spider-Man can't fly, right?"

Victoria looked ready to claw him. "Enough!"

"No, I mean, because there was a flying man," he said defensively. "I mean, I didn't see him, but our pilot said–"

"There was no flying man," I insisted. Then I explained to Victoria, "Our pilot said he saw a flying knight or something, but we didn't see a thing. My theory is he sprinkled something special on those hoagies."

"Hoagies?!" Our Leader cut in. "Why are we talking about hoagies and flying men? What is all of this even about? I never authorized any poisonous milk. This is all a hoax concocted by the media!"

"Sir," I said gently, "don't you remember Project Milkman?"

"Project Milkman? But that's not what the milk is supposed to do!" He thrust a pudgy finger at the angry townsfolk on TV. "I wanted zombies, not...*zombies*!"

"So, Crisis Communications 101 would say to be fully transparent about what happened. Say we made a mistake and explain how we're going to fix it."

Our Leader gave me a death stare.

Scott saw it and burst out laughing. "Good one, Blake!"

Victoria giggled, Debbie snorted, and finally Our Leader joined in. "Oh, you're joking!" bleated the President. "How rich!"

I forced myself to laugh, too.

Our Leader cackled. "And to think I was about to order you dead!"

I gulped, but the President kept laughing. "Now I'm the one who's joking! Or am I? No, I am. Actually, I'm not! No, no, I am, I am. Wow, your face is priceless right now!"

"Look," I said, trying to recover. "All I'm saying is that with this video out there, we can't just deny the whole thing. Our only choice is to hold a press conference and spin this in our favor."

"I agree with Blake," said Scott, reliable as always. "But we don't have a Press Secretary. Who's going to go out there?"

Holding press conferences had been the job of Rico, last seen kicking and screaming in the arms of Our

Leader's guards. While he was something of a sourpuss off-screen, Rico was a good-looking guy with enough charm to handle a whole pit of snakes. Scott and I were more suited to staying behind the scenes, like co-directors of a grand propaganda film.

"What if we sent out Victoria?" suggested Scott, who clearly had been thinking through the same conundrum.

"I'm your boss," she reminded him. "You can't send me anywhere. Anyway, it won't be necessary." She tapped a button on her phone and said, "Bring up Rico."

Scott and I were dumbfounded. Rico was...OK?

Our Leader yawned. "Well, back to the Throne Room for me. I've got to take a shit."

We held polite smiles until the odious man had gone.

"Which throne do you think he meant?" asked Scott.

Rico entered the room, escorted by a guard. He looked fresh as a daisy. The kid was even grinning, an expression I hadn't seen on his face since his first day on the job. "Hey, guys!" he greeted brightly.

"Rico," Scott said slowly, "are you... Is everything...?"

"Never been better! Sorry, I got so *cranky* yesterday. What was that about? Hah!"

I blinked. "But...where have you been?"

"Just downstairs," Rico said like it was no big thing. "Actually? It was really great for me."

I wasn't sure I wanted to know more, so I put the matter aside and got to work writing Rico a humdinger of an opening statement for the press conference.

Cameras clicked like crickets as Rico stepped up to the

podium. We had him wearing jeans with a sports coat over a royal blue T-shirt, a look that emphasized his youthfulness and made him look more like the founder of a tech startup than a government employee. Standing in front of a calming blue backdrop with a subtle flag pattern, Rico flashed a set of pearly whites.

I was sitting in the Comms Situation Room. Leaning into a microphone that linked to a tiny speaker in Rico's ear, I said, "OK now, Rico, just read slowly and take as much time as you need. Your statement should leave only five minutes for questions. I'll be right here to help you dodge any screwballs."

I pressed a button to activate the teleprompter.

"Hey, folks," read Rico. "Oh hey, I see Joan from WARK Radio is here. You were on vacation, right?"

"Joan's not back yet," someone said.

"Good to see you, Joan," Rico continued to read. "Who else is here? Or maybe I should ask, who isn't here? We've got a full house! We really appreciate your patriotism, coming here, asking questions, fulfilling your civic duty as reporters. It's just great to see. Really great to see. Really, really great to—"

"Rico, could you please explain something to me?" interrupted John Sexton, an impetuous young journalist from the *Capital Post*. He'd quickly moved up the chain at the newspaper, which annoyed me since the place had refused to give me an interview when I was starting out. Sexton's uncle was the publisher, so I had to assume that nepotism was involved.

"Don't take the question," I growled into my mic. "Finish the opening statement."

"Now, John," said Rico in a slightly hurt tone. "I'll get

to everybody's questions in just a bit. But I want to do my opening statement first, which might even answer your question. If that's all right with you?"

"Of course," replied Sexton, biting his lip. It was good to have Rico back. A lot of the reporters seemed to have a real hard-on for the guy. It was as if they really didn't want him to be mad at them. Neither did the reporters' bosses, who saw any significant tension with the government as bad for business.

"Thanks, John," said the Press Secretary. "But before I get to that, I just wanted to give a few thank-yous…"

We were back on track. Holding a press conference is a great tool for projecting transparency without actually providing any useful information. As long as the government provides the opportunity to ask questions, it doesn't have to answer any of them.

The thank-you section of Rico's remarks went on for about five minutes. Brilliantly, I'd included a lengthy anecdote about the one-hundredth birthday of a woman who fought in two wars and then survived a terror attack, the kind of story no reporter would dare interrupt. It was even true for the most part.

"All right, so let's get down to brass tacks," said Rico, continuing to read the teleprompter. I liked lines that implied serious business was afoot. "I'm sure you've all seen the so-called footage from Chesterville." *So-called* was another of my favorite terms.

Rico held out his hands. "Believe me, nobody was more troubled than Our Leader when he saw what *appeared* to be one of our great communities portrayed in the media as drugged and violent. As you know, Our Leader abhors drugs and abhors violence. That's why one of his first executive orders was to put together the Addiction to Dangerous and Harmful Drugs Task Force. The ADHD Task Force, I'm happy to report, is set to release a white paper in the coming weeks or months with a series of sensible recommendations on how we might be able to tackle this national crisis. This is a national crisis, and believe me, Chesterville's going to get the help and treatment it deserves."

John Sexton then blurted, "Hasn't there been criticism of the ADHD Task Force's ability to focus on—"

"Now, John, I think Marguerite had her hand up," said Rico. "So we'll get to you a little bit later, OK? Marguerite?"

Marguerite Susquehanna was from *Hawk News*, an overtly conservative alternative news network to Triple N. Like most women on that channel, she had blonde hair and an eye-popping figure. She had nothing on Maria, though.

Marguerite asked, "Are you saying what we saw in Chesterville wasn't a big-government program to—?"

"Let me stop you right there, Margo." Rico took a swig of water as he waited for me to come up with a response.

"Nothing in that video..." I said into his ear.

"Nothing in that video," he repeated, "shows anything resembling a government program. In fact, that video leaves a lot of open questions. We've been told it's Chesterville, sure, but there's no way to know that for sure. We don't even know if Chesterville is a real town!"

"Now hang on a second, Ricky," interjected Barbara Goldstein from the *Global Inquirer*.

Uh oh, I thought. Babs was an old-school scooper. She was a reporter back when reporters reported. I wished she'd just retire already. "Quick, Rico, take an easy question from Abdul!"

"Hold on, Babs," said Rico. "Abdul has been waiting a while to ask a question. Abdul?"

"Thank you, Mr. Fuentes," said Abdul Osmani, the ever-pleased foreign-press reporter. "When will Our Leader visit the beautiful kingdom of—"

"Ricky," interrupted Babs, plowing ahead with her question. She was studying a wire-bound paper notebook through a thick pair of reading glasses. "Just a minute ago you said, and I quote, 'Chesterville's going to get the help and treatment it needs.' Why would you say that if Our Leader believes this video isn't Chesterville, or that Chesterville isn't even a real town?"

Crap. She had a point. I needed to stall.

"I never said Chesterville isn't a real town," I said, and Rico regurgitated.

"You said, and I quote, 'We don't even know if Chesterville is a real town.'"

"Semantics," I said.

"Semantics," he repeated. "Next?"

Not surprisingly, Babs didn't stand down. "You haven't answered my question."

"Uh," said Rico.

I found myself at a loss, too, and said, "Hold on, let me make something up."

"Hold on," echoed Rico, "let me make something up."

"Pardon?" replied Babs with deep offense. "You're making this up?"

I must have screamed, because Rico tore the speaker out of his ear. "Let me show you something," he told the reporters, suddenly going rogue. His hand disappeared inside the podium and he fumbled around for something—I didn't know what. Sometimes we put props down there, but I hadn't given Rico anything for show-and-tell. For a cold second, I thought he might have a gun. To my relief—but also my confusion—he pulled out a glass of milk.

"This is the milk in question," the Press Secretary declared, holding it out in front of him for the cameras to flash. "Cheers." And he drank it, all of it, in one long chug. "Ah, that's good. And see? No ill effects."

Barbara looked too stunned to ask a follow-up question. It was brilliant. Rico was brilliant. It was going to work!

Rico closed his eyes like he was absorbing a particularly good afternoon sun on the beach. Then he swayed to the right and fell over sideways.

CHAPTER
TWELVE

N o, Rico wasn't dead, but he was most certainly asleep. The guards took him back to wherever they had been keeping him. I didn't ask where. I don't have to lie about things I didn't know.

Anyway, it was fairly obvious what had happened. I'd been suspicious of the curmudgeonly Press Secretary's sudden perkiness and general good humor from the start. Someone must have had made him taste one, or perhaps a mixture, of the milk samples we'd brought back to the Compound. The drug had worked for a little while to level off Rico's worst qualities, but then an overdose during the press conference had knocked him out completely.

The rest of us looked pretty ragged sitting around the conference table in the Situation Room. I stuffed my face with stale donuts as Debbie talked our ears off about the dire social consequences of Rico's stage dive.

Scott sat up in his chair. "Wait, why would there be mimes?"

"Not mimes," Debbie replied with some exasperation. "Memes!"

"Well, *excuse* me for not speaking *en français*."

Debbie looked to Victoria for help. "Do I really have to explain what a meme is?"

"Please don't," our boss replied without looking up from her laptop. "Those of us who are not one hundred years old understand."

"Hey," Scott replied defensively.

"The best case is that everyone on the Internet is going to think Rico is hilarious," I said, hoping to simplify the issue for my friend. "Worst case, they're going to use this as evidence that the milk is sour."

"The hashtag #SpilledMilk is trending," Debbie said gravely. "So, worst case."

What really stunk was that Rico's pratfall had ruined what otherwise could have been an epic save. Barbara Goldstein's story in the *Global Inquirer* referred to the Press Secretary's reaction as "curdling the whole milk affair." It was an impressive pun, and I had to laugh, but it was not the kind of headline we wanted Our Leader to read.

I did feel a *little* to blame. I mean, I had choked big time when old Babs asked about the contradictory statements. It was a rookie mistake to make contradictory arguments, especially at the same press conference. It always worked better to keep things simple—make a good line and stick to it. It was weird because I didn't usually make mistakes like that. The truth was that I'd been feeling a bit off my game ever since the hound pounced on us a few days ago.

Victoria looked concerned. "What's wrong with you, Ham-ner? You look like shit."

I winced. Not only because of the profane word, but because she knew perfectly well how to say my name. In retrospect, maybe this was revenge for me forgetting hers. "The *n* is silent."

Victoria smiled slightly. "Well, the shit is loud."

Scott burst out laughing. "Sorry, Hamner, but that was pretty good."

"Sorry if I'm breaking your cute little non-cursing rule," she said with a wink. Victoria shut the laptop with some finality and got up from her seat. "I'm going to the Rose Garden to dig us out of this mess. I've just agreed to beam into Maria's show."

Scott roused from listlessness. "Are you sure that's a good idea? You don't have...*any* experience talking to the press. At least take an earpiece so Blake and I can guide you through any tough questions."

She scoffed. "Uh, no thank you. I think we all saw how well that worked at the press conference."

We had a camera in the Rose Garden with a line to the TV news stations so that they could videoconference us into their coverage. It was easier than driving to a studio, and it let us maintain a little more control over the interview. We could always fake technical difficulties if things started going south.

Since we weren't invited to come out and watch, and anyway no one really wanted to stand out in the cold, Scott, Debbie, and I stayed in the Comms Situation Room and watched the interview on TV. Wearing a thick gray fur coat, Victoria somewhat resembled a wolf, but the look in her eyes was more like a deer in the headlights.

"Hi, Maria!" she shouted much too loudly.

Maria winced. "We can hear you just fine. No need to speak up."

Victoria blushed slightly. "Sorry, I'm a bit new at this!"

"And you already have a crisis on your hands."

I chuckled. Maria was good.

Victoria frowned. "That's not fair, Maria. I don't see any...*crisis*...as you put it."

"Well, what would you call it?"

"There's nothing here I would call anything."

"Sorry? I'm not sure I understand..."

"You wouldn't name a cat 'Puss' if there was no cat, would you?"

Scott and I exchanged looks. This certainly seemed like a new strategy.

Maria squinted. "So, are you saying that you don't think there's any cause for outrage that the government is experimenting—"

"—Allegedly—"

"—on citizens of this country by drugging their milk? Tell me, Veronica, when are you planning to expand this pilot project to the rest of the country?"

"Look, Maria, I didn't come on here to talk about unsubstantiated reports from terrorists."

"Terrorists? You're saying the video came from a terrorist?"

"It caused terror, yes? Do you feel safe? I sure don't. But the good news is that we have a terror task force that's doing a really bang-up job finding the terrorists and bringing them to justice. In fact—and I'm guessing this is new information for you—we've already identified the source."

I glanced at Scott. "Did we identify the source?"

He shrugged wildly. "Don't look at me!"

Maria looked aghast. "Who's the source?"

Victoria smiled. "It's nice of you to cover for him, but you don't need to pretend not to know any longer. The video came from Jetpack."

Maria raised an eyebrow. "I'm sorry?"

"Certainly you've seen his stickers all around town? Jetpack and his followers are terrorists."

I'm not sure I would have equated decals with terror. It was hard to tell if she was exaggerating or making the accusation out of whole cloth. I mean, those sticker jockeys had always been a nuisance, but this would be a pretty big move. If it was true—and I didn't put it past Victoria to lie to the media—when did she find out and why didn't she tell us?

Maria placed a finger to her earpiece. "I'm getting word that—yes, we can now confirm that we received the video from someone named Jetpack." She turned to Victoria. "But what makes you say this is terror?"

My question exactly!

"Oh, come on, Maria. Didn't this video make you feel scared?"

"But that was because—"

Victoria shook a fist. "We're not going to let the Jetpacks undermine the rule of law, or—let me add— our strong economy. We've also got—as Rico mentioned in his press conference, which perhaps you would have reported if you knew how to do your job—"

"Excuse me?" protested Maria.

"Ouch," I said, sucking air through my teeth.

"Don't interrupt me," my boss snapped. "I took your questions and now you're going to take my answers."

The directness stunned Maria into silence. Victoria then continued.

"Appreciate it. Now, as I was trying to say, we're going to have this really great anti-drug program that's going to help the people of Chesterville get better. And by the way, what about all the jobs we're creating here? Milkmen have been out of work for decades! Let me tell you, Maria, those people aren't outraged. They're positively ecstatic about this project."

Maria blinked. "I don't know what I want to ask first. Are...are the people of Chesterville addicted to—are you admitting the milk is an addictive drug?"

"I'm not *admitting* anything, Maria." Victoria winked as if she'd just put one over on my wife. I knew from my years of marriage to Maria thinking that was always a mistake. "But, uh, I think it's pretty clear from the video that they're addicted."

"You mean it's pretty clear from the video that you just said was fake? The video you said was produced by terrorists?"

Victoria rolled her eyes, seemingly unfazed that another reporter had called out the contradiction. "We've already addressed this question a hundred times. Why don't we talk about something that matters for once, like how Our Leader has reduced the unemployment rate by 2.1 percent since he's taken office? People don't care about drugs and terror, Maria. They care about jobs. And milkmen have been suffering especially. Remember how wonderful things were when there was door-to-door milk service? And how sweet that milk tasted? Gosh!"

"You were the one talking about drugs and terror."

"Enough doom and gloom, Maria. Let's talk about jobs!"

"OK, fine, let's talk about jobs. You're saying that a nationwide rollout of this milk, which Chesterville is so addicted to that you need to send in anti-drug specialists, is going to...bring back milk delivery as an industry?"

"Well, I wouldn't say it exactly like *that*, but yes. Jobs, jobs, jobs. And don't forget, the anti-drug specialists are jobs, too. This is win-win-win."

"Wait, what's the third win?"

"All of us," said Victoria. "We win."

Maria glanced toward the camera with a gentle raise of the eyebrows and slight widening of the mouth. It was my wife's trademark signal to her audience that she was fully aware her interview subject was a complete wacko. I had to chuckle.

Scott gaped at me as the show went to commercial. "That was..."

"Awful," I said with perhaps a little too much mirth. Victoria brought it out in me.

He shook his head. "No, no, I think—I mean, it was confusing as hell, but maybe that's what we needed. Give everyone a headache so they move on to something else."

"*Jetpack* is trending," reported Debbie. "Social sentiment is...curious."

"How so?" asked Scott.

"No, I mean, people are curious about him."

I really did have a migraine.

A bell chimed that made Scott and I turn with sheer terror to Debbie. Her face turned several shades greener as she read her phone. Our Leader was woozing.

"What did he say?" I demanded.

She passed the device to me. It was bad.

The social guru stammered, "We have to get out there and warn her!"

I gulped. "I don't think we have enough time. We could shut down the camera before the show comes back from break."

Scott shook his head and pointed at the screen as a *Breaking News* banner flashed across the screen. "We're too late!"

Maria turned to the camera. "We're still here with Victoria Chu, Communications Director for Our Leader. Sorry, I think I may have called you Veronica in the last segment. Anyway, the President just said some pretty interesting things on Woozler."

Victoria blinked. "Oh?"

"Our Leader writes, 'The milk is my gift to make you happier. I just want everyone to be happier, so we're going to bring the milk to the entire country as soon as we work out the kinks. You're going to love it.'"

Victoria fell instantly into a coughing fit, a common tactic that PR newbies employed to buy time.

"This seems to contradict a lot of what you just told us, Victoria. Care to explain?"

"I don't think it's very fair of you to spring this on me, Maria."

Now my wife looked really annoyed. "Victoria, I didn't spring this on you. Your boss did."

"I think you're taking what he said out of context."

"Out of context? That was an exact quote!"

"No, it's not, because he's going to say more soon. Let's allow the context to develop before dissecting—"

"Excuse me? Allow the context to develop?"

"What? Hey, Maria? I think...I think I'm losing reception. Can you hear me?"

That was the cue for us to fake a connectivity problem and end the videoconference. For a second, I thought about leaving Victoria hanging, but then decided I should think of serving my true boss, the President. I hit a button and Victoria vanished from the TV.

"Too bad we can't do that when she's standing right in front of us," said Scott, dry as a towel.

CHAPTER
THIRTEEN

T HE MEDIA CONTINUED to slurp the milk story the next day and through Wednesday morning. Our denials were not making the story go away, and it was clear we needed a fresh strategy.

When it's no longer credible to deny, the only remaining option is to divert. Scott and I realized in the early days of the administration that Our Leader would face such a crisis, so we'd brainstormed a little something called the "Grand List of Distractions."

I searched my desk and couldn't find it. Just as I was about to blow a fuse, Scott discovered the document on the floor of my closet, hiding under a pair of starch-white sneakers that were supposed to encourage me to go to the Compound's gym—wherever the heck that was. Giddy with anticipation, I blew off the dust and held the parchment in the light.

1. Accuse previous president of infidelity.
2. Fire the Vice President.
3. Accuse international ally of wiretapping Our Leader.
4. Zoo prison break!
5. Threaten to bomb an insignificant country.
6. Reveal nationwide outbreak of food poisoning.

7. Announce Our Leader is getting married.
8. Require businesspeople to wear hats like in the old days.
9. Bacon festival, with free bacon!
10. False alarm air raid / missile crisis
11. Announce national music contest judged by Our Leader.

I frowned slightly at a circular stain on the page that was the exact circumference of a beer bottle. These ideas weren't nearly as smart as I had remembered.

"Ooh, infidelity," said Scott, reading over my shoulder. He whistled. "Wait, we tried that one already, right?"

I nodded. "Nobody actually cared." I crossed that one out, as well as the one about firing the Veep, which had been a much more successful distraction.

Our Leader fired Vice President Antonia Daniels in week two. It had precipitated a big debate over whether the President could in fact fire the Vice President, which we turned into an even larger debate over what the Vice President actually did, which naturally led people to ask if it was really necessary to have one at all. The Speaker of the House, who had either forgotten she was next in the chain of succession or simply preferred her current position, argued against having a vice president and convinced her colleagues to make the position optional. This quickly ended any possible discussion of finding a replacement, which to be honest would have been a huge headache. But the best part was that, by the end of the two-week story, everyone had forgotten all about Our Leader's extremely offensive remarks about Paralympians.

The (former) Vice President had been fine with the

whole thing. She'd never really wanted the job in the first place, but as a moderate woman with nearly forty years of Senate experience, Antonia had nicely balanced Our Leader on the ballot. Having served that purpose, all the old prune had really been doing in the executive branch was ribbon cuttings and a lot of cocaine. Shortly after the firing, Daniels got a book deal. I hadn't seen the book yet, but hey—one crisis at a time.

"I don't see any of these ideas working," I said, shaking my head. "Were we drunk when we wrote this?"

Scott looked offended. "Hey, don't spit on the Grand List. This is a great list, and it doesn't matter what we did or didn't drink to inspire it."

I groaned.

"Well, if you don't want to do any of these, couldn't you just ask Maria to make up something? Tell her you'll pay her back with a nice island vacation."

"You know about our rule," I reminded him. "Anyway, I already promised Maria that trip."

"You mean your honeymoon? Jesus, Blake, it's been how many years since the wedding?"

"I know, I know..."

"Because of this job?" He sounded guilty.

"Well, and her job."

Sharing the blame with Triple N seemed to make Scott feel better. "Yeah, I bet that network must run her thin."

I returned my attention to the Grand List. Stupidity wasn't the only problem with a lot of the ideas; it was their potential cost. Our Leader had been getting a little tight with the budget lately and I wasn't sure how many of these ideas we could do on the cheap.

"If only a celebrity would die," commented my colleague.

Such a lucky stroke had gotten us out of a previous crisis. Our Leader had announced a gun buyback program and *joked* that people who refused to sell back their guns would be shot with them. Neither supporters nor opponents of gun control found that very funny. Things were spiraling out of control, but then pop star Percy Penn drank too much at a mansion party, slipped down some marble stairs, and impaled himself on a Roman statue. The news cycle completely flipped from Our Leader's flub to Percy's perforation.

Yes, there were some conspiracy nuts who had theorized that the President had wanted the heartthrob dead because they'd been engaged in a Woozler feud ever since Penn beat Our Leader's record for most platinum albums. But I swear we had nothing to do with it! The truth was that the fight had further boosted the singer's profile, and he thanked Our Leader behind the scenes with a big cash contribution to the President's reelection campaign. We certainly had nothing against the man.

We should have thrown out the list and—soberly— come up with some new ideas, but I was still feeling mentally blocked in the wake of the hound attack, and I was just getting so sick of the milk story.

"Maybe the fake missile crisis?" I suggested. "That would be quick and wouldn't cost that much, right?"

Scott looked at me as if I was an idiot. "How much do you think missiles cost?"

"We don't have to actually fire a missile," I explained. "All we have to do is blast out an alert, wait a few minutes, then announce it was a false alarm."

A grinning Scott called out, "Can I get a *whoop-whoop* for the Hammer?"

"Whoop-whoop!" called out Debbie from behind us, shocking the living daylights out of me.

"How long have you been standing there?" I demanded.

Either she didn't want to say, or she was too involved in her phone to hear the question. "I'd recommend you do it soon. Hashtag #VitaminDemented is really catching fire today on Woozler."

"Huh?" asked Scott, frowning. "Well, I'd give you the sign off, but I'm not in charge, anymore. Should we run it by Victoria?"

This probably would have been the sensible thing to do, but I was tired of dealing with our new boss's bullcrap. "No, let's just do it. Scott, you'll need to call Homeland Security, but first—Debbie, I need you to lay a little foundation."

Laying foundation meant setting up a possible scapegoat in case the plan went awry.

"Sure," she chirped. "What do you want me to wooze?"

"Thank Dr. Norbert Falz for all the great work he's been doing on emergency alerts."

"On it."

Scott got on the phone to order the alarm. About a minute later, all our phones lit up, beeping with rising panic. A message on the screen read: *Missile attack imminent! Take cover immediately!* People received the warning across the country, which I knew wasn't realistic, but didn't really matter.

Scott and I—the pranksters—started laughing hysterically. And it really did all seem to be in good fun until we switched on the TV. The image punched me hard in the gut: Maria afraid.

"...and...and to my husband, Blake: If...if you're watching this, I j-just want you to know that I love you so much and...and...I'm sorry that I'm not there with you right now..."

What had I done? I should have warned Maria. No, no, I couldn't have warned her. She's on the news. If I had told her, she would have had to tell the truth on TV or else we'd be breaking the rule.

The truth was, I shouldn't have done it in the first place. If only I had been thinking straight. What had that stupid hound done to me?

I shook Scott by the shoulders.

"Hey, stop that."

"We have to stop this!" I howled.

"Calm down, would you?" He checked his golden Rolex. "The correction should be coming any second now."

Everyone's phone beeped again with a new message: *False alarm! No missile. Have a nice day.*

I turned back to Maria on the TV screen. She looked up from her phone with disbelief, then disappointment. "False alarm," announced the anchor, pausing to collect her thoughts. "After the break, we're going to get to the bottom of what happened, how it happened, and how *he* could have let this happen." Maria pointed to an image of Our Leader's Compound that appeared prominently in the set behind her seat.

Most viewers probably thought she was referring to

Our Leader, but I was pretty sure she was talking about me.

"This isn't good," I mumbled. "I'm such an idiot."

"Yay!" cheered Debbie. "Hashtag #FalseAlarm is trending! Just above #OhGodWhy, #LastWords and...well, the next few get a little profane."

So, we'd mopped up the milk with a missile. I would still have to clean up the fallout at home.

CHAPTER
FOURTEEN

MARIA BARELY SPOKE to me for the rest of the week. It was worse than anger—she just seemed so...disappointed in me, I guess. I thought one evening I'd find the time to stop at the grocery store and buy ingredients to make us a nice coq au vin, just like the old days, but I never got around to cooking because I had to work late every night spinning the fake missile crisis.

Maria and I didn't even really see each other until Saturday morning, when we had to rush out of the house to make it on time to our niece Paula's birthday party. My brother, Randy, and his family live out in the suburbs. It's not that long of a trip, but having snowed overnight, it took us about an hour just to get out of the city. To keep things interesting, I turned off our white hover sedan's self-driving mode and didn't use the GPS. It felt good to regain control.

Upon reaching the highway, I switched on the radio to listen to Defense Secretary Emmanuel Strachatto, who I'd suggested putting on the air to field questions about the false alarm. We'd gotten hit hard with negative media coverage. While no one had figured out that we'd intentionally faked the whole thing, we still looked pretty dang incompetent.

The good thing about Strachatto was that reporters

usually struggled to find the courage to ask him any tough questions. They just respected the five-star general too darn much. Gentle questions required gentle answers, so I'd personally trained Strachatto to spin by deploying a "You're right" defense in interviews.

"But...General...sir...," stammered the hapless radio reporter. "You do understand the alarm it caused when people thought that they and their loved ones were about to perish?"

"You're right, you're absolutely right," said Strachatto in that crackly baritone that was so pleasing to the ears. "However, I'd like to point out that if there had truly been an incoming missile, the fact we have this wireless alert system shows that citizens would have had plenty of warning. And the fact that this came as such a surprise to everyone shows, I think, how effective our troops have been overseas in preventing attacks on the homeland. So, I think we should all take a moment to thank our troops for their extraordinary service."

Finding moments to thank the troops was another tactic I'd taught the general.

Maria huffed. "I don't want to listen to this. It's the weekend. Can we please leave work at work for once?"

I turned it off. "OK. Well, do you want to talk or something?"

She said she wanted to listen to a podcast, so rather than communicate we learned ten strange facts about kale. I found it interesting to learn that too much kale can cause hypothyroidism—but held back repeating this to my health-conscious wife.

I began to regret not using the car's navigation features when we entered Randy's neighborhood of identical McMansions and streets named after similar-sounding fruit. To get to his house, we had to take Blackberry Boulevard to Blueberry Circle, then take the second right onto Boysenberry Avenue. The house itself wasn't too difficult to locate thanks to all the minivans parked along the street. The vehicles were plastered with various bumper stickers, including school logos, stick-figure families, and fish—both for Jesus and Darwin.

I raised my eyebrows at Maria. "Looks like we could be in for a Christian/Atheist debate."

My wife failed to even acknowledge the comment. I know I'm not *that* funny, but when I can't even get a half smile out of my love, it's pretty clear I'm in deep trouble.

I parked the car and we got out. Maria reached into the backseat for a big box wrapped in golden paper and headed straight to the house without saying anything. I felt as if I was chasing her up the walk. My brother opened the door just as I arrived at her side.

"You made it," said Randy with a grin. He'd put on a clean shirt for once, but my older brother still looked as harried as the day his daughter was born. "Paula, look who's here!"

My niece took one look and squealed, "Unkie Blake and Aunt Maria!"

Paula had her black hair in braids and was dressed like a warrior princess. I couldn't believe she was turning seven. It felt like only days earlier that she'd been cradled in my arms, smiling about a really good fart.

"I'm not your uncle," I said, gnarling my lips. My fingers curled into mangled claws. "I am...the Winter Beast!"

Shrieking giddily, Paula struck me in the leg with her sword. As I feigned a fall to my knees, she ran back to play with her friends, who were also wearing medieval costumes and wielding plastic wands and swords.

Something crashed in the kitchen. "Oh no, that's Bo," said Randy. That was our five-year-old nephew. My brother leaped into action, leaving Maria and I to fend for ourselves.

"I'm going out to vape," stated Maria, dropping the heavy golden gift into my hands. I wasn't actually sure what was inside the box. My wife had ordered it online and wrapped it one night when I was working late at the office.

I watched the TV anchor walk out the glass door into the backyard to vape an electronic death stick in the cold.

I lowered the present onto a small open space on Randy's dining room table. There were a few other adults standing around the pile. They seemed to be discussing the pros and cons of hover technology in baby strollers, so I grabbed a seat by myself on Randy's blue sofa and got out my phone. I checked for work e-mails, then moved on to Woozler to find out what was trending. It was still the missile crisis.

A shadow fell over me. "Blake, if you don't put down that phone, I swear I will flush it down the toilet." Bouncing onto the sofa, Randy gave me a playful, yet still painful, punch to the shoulder.

With a sarcastic wink, I shut off the screen and stuck the phone in my pocket. "What do you want me to do?"

"Talk to some people!" he exclaimed, motioning toward the other adults in the room. "Have a beer!"

Grumbling, I rose to my feet and moseyed over to a small group of parents who seemed to be discussing the missile warning. I figured that if I couldn't do reconnaissance on my device, I might as well try to do it face-to-face.

"I left work straightaway to get Darla from school," one mother declared, then laughed. "Grant got there at the exact same time!"

Grant, apparently Darla's dad, tipped an invisible hat to the rest of us. "I'd also left work straightaway. Come to think of it, half the office must have done the same that day."

The other parents chuckled knowingly.

He winked. "You know, I might have even beat Viv there..."

This got guffaws.

"Oh, Grant, it's not a competition."

Uck. Parents are the worst.

"So," I said. The parents turned as if seeing me for the first time. "What do you think happened?"

They didn't know I worked for Our Leader. I usually introduced myself as "working in communications," and left it at that.

Another mother, whose name I'd forgotten, cocked her eyes traitorously and whispered, "I heard there was a scientist who pressed the wrong button."

She said "scientist" as if that was a crime in itself. This meant our messaging on science was working. I wasn't quite clear, though, why she felt the need to make the whole thing sound like a secret. After all, she was merely repeating the explanation we'd fed the press.

John Sexton of the *Capitol Post* had picked up on Debbie's wooze thanking Dr. Falz for his work on emergency alerts and asked us if the scientist was involved. We didn't say he was, but we also didn't deny it. We let Sexton fill in the blanks and didn't go out of our way to correct him. The truth was that Falz didn't work anywhere near homeland security, but the *Post* report seemed plausible because no one liked scientists. So, Falz took the fall for the false alarm. Ingeniously, we paired his subsequent dismissal with the unveiling of a new and improved warning system. Featuring cutting edge AI, it would require no person—scientist or otherwise—to operate the system. All we needed was someone to figure out how to build it.

I was glad the parents seemed pleased with the government's resolution of the false alarm, because in the first few hours, Maria had been pushing for an investigation of what went wrong. I'm pretty sure she knew the whole thing was just a distraction from the botched Milkman effort, but she couldn't find anyone to admit it, and as an objective news anchor she wasn't supposed to give her opinion.

One of the dad's phones beeped. With a gasp at the screen, he blurted, "Ava's heart rate just increased ten points! I better go check on her."

The fool darted toward a little girl happily chasing Paula around the table, wrapped his arms around her and made her take a timeout on the floor. Ava began bawling.

"We used one of those vitals apps for our first kid," commented Grant.

His wife, Viv, shrugged. "But we didn't even discuss using it for Darla."

That got some laughs, too. Grant and Viv were a real riot.

"So, which one's yours?" asked Grant.

"Huh?" I replied, realizing a few seconds late he was addressing me.

He motioned toward the children. "Who's your kid?"

"Oh, I...uh..." For some reason, this question always made me stammer. "I'm just Paula and Bo's uncle."

"Oh," said Grant with a smirk. "Well, enjoy the freedom while you still can!"

His disapproving wife put her hands on her hips. "Grant..."

"Just kidding, honey."

Laughing, she leaned toward me and whispered, "No, he's right. Enjoy it while you can."

I strained a smile, then turned my attention to the kids. Paula was reaching for a bowl of candy on the dining room table. Her five-year-old brother rocked up and tugged at her dress.

"Go away, Bo!" snapped Paula, pushing him to the floor.

Bo emitted a sound somewhere between wolf howl and smoke detector siren.

"What happened?!" yowled Randy, pouncing at his litter.

To my niece's credit, Paula didn't lose her cool. "I was helping Bo get some candy from the table, and he just...fell over," she said. Paula reached for a lollipop and handed it to her crying brother. "Here, Bo."

He stopped crying, smiled as though nothing was ever wrong, and took the candy.

My niece was one-fifth my age but appeared ready to take my job.

Randy, who wasn't very good at detecting his children's lies, positively beamed. "You're a very good sister."

I slow-clapped. "End scene. Bravo."

Randy gave me a funny look. "What?"

"Oh, nothing." I figured I wouldn't betray my niece on her own birthday. Maybe I'd help Bo get revenge at his next party.

Taking me aside, Randy whispered, "So what's going on with you and Maria, anyway?"

"What do you mean?"

He raised an eyebrow. "You guys haven't been in the same room this whole time. Anyway, Maria is the one who's usually more social."

I glanced out the back door at my wife. She was sitting on a chair by herself in the garden.

"Nothing," I said. "You know, work stuff."

"Yours or hers?"

I didn't respond and Randy *tsk-tsk*ed. He loved to remind me he was older and wiser. "The job's getting to be too much, Blake. You should be starting a family. That's never going to happen if—"

"Yeah, yeah, I get the point, OK? I'm not going to be there forever. I'm just looking for the right time."

He raised his eyebrows doubtfully. "You said the same thing at Paula's last birthday. It's going to be another new year in a couple days."

"I know."

"Any New Year's Eve plans?"

"I've got to work."

"Seriously? Why don't you spend it with Maria?"

"Maria's working, too. She's hosting again for Triple N."

Randy shook his head. I kind of wanted to punch him. "Go apologize to your wife, Blake," he said.

"You don't even know that it was my fault!" I protested. Now I really wanted to punch him.

"Would you tell me if I asked?"

"Er, no. It's...confidential."

"But you need to apologize for something, right?"

I sighed. "Yeah..."

He clapped me on the back. "So, go do it."

"Where's *your* wife hiding, anyway?"

Randy looked stunned. "She *left* me, Blake."

My eyes must have bugged out, because Randy couldn't keep a straight face and burst out laughing. "Just messing with you, man. She's got a headache, so I told her to lie down upstairs. Jesus, maybe if you didn't work so much, you would know what was going on with us."

"Is...is something going on?"

"No! That's my whole point. Look, don't change the subject. Go make up with Maria. I want the two of you to be Paula's inseparable aunt and uncle before cake time."

"But..."

He turned away and called to the children, "Who wants candy?"

I decided I would go out back, if nothing else than to escape the kids' exhilarated screams. There was snow on the ground, but the cool air felt good. I found Maria sitting on a white-iron lawn chair, looking glamorous in the cream wool coat that she often wore for long outdoor shoots. Clutching a silver e-cigarette, my wife stared with great concentration into the empty distance, as if trying to make sense of a challenging abstract painting.

"I'm sorry," I said.

"For what?" she asked without turning her head toward me.

"I know you got scared by the whole missile thing."

After a long silence, she asked, "Was it real?"

"You reported it was a false alarm," I pointed out. "We never said that was wrong."

"I'm not asking if our reporting is accurate. I'm asking when you knew it was a false alarm."

I watched my boots gather moisture in the snow. "I'm not sure I understand..."

"Did you plan the false alarm, Blake?"

You know that airless feeling you get when you get hit right in the gut? Like you can't breathe? That's how I felt. "You know I can't talk about that. Our rule..."

Maria cut me off with a deep blow of steam from her luscious lips. While I didn't like Maria's addiction to vaping, I had to admit she sure looked cool doing it. "You know, my new bosses have been asking me about your job. Our relationship was never an issue before, but now suddenly there's more scrutiny at Triple N over potential conflicts of interest."

"Did you tell them about our rule?"

She nodded. "They said we'd have a larger discussion later. I had to deal with the breaking news, so that kind of put it off."

"Hey, so maybe the false alarm wasn't all bad, right?"

Maria gave me a look that wiped the grin right off my face.

"I was scared, Blake." She said. "And I don't think you understand why."

I pulled up another lawn chair. "You thought...we weren't going to see each other again?"

"It was more than that," she said, wiping away a tear. "I just saw our future...I don't know...blink out."

I thought that was what I'd said.

Perhaps reading my mind, she replied, "It's not the same thing. Blake, this... I don't want this to be it. There's so much more I want for us before we die. Do you understand what I'm saying to you?"

"I know you think I should quit, and I want to, but I think if I can just hold out a little longer, it will really give me a good foundation to—"

Maria stopped me with a cold stare. "You're not this stupid, Blake. You know I'm not talking about your job. Although, yes, you should quit."

I guess I must have felt cornered, because at this point base PR instincts took over. "Well, while we're on the topic of quitting before we die young, maybe you should give up vaping."

For the record, this was "Attack, attack, attack," a strategy whereby one changes the subject by lobbing bombs at the interviewer. While often effective, if does not often leave you in the other person's good graces. I especially do not recommend using it on one's spouse, as I was doing now.

"I'll quit," Maria hissed, "when you're ready to be a fucking adult."

The glass door slid open right on the profanity, with Paula and some other kids running out in cute winter coats.

"A fudging adult," Maria corrected herself, needlessly.

I was about to respond when something cold exploded white against my arm. I turned and saw that grinning little devil Paula gathering her next snowball.

"What have you done?" I cried to the children. Deepening my voice, I roared, "You have awoken the Winter Beast!"

I tromped toward the kids like a big, slow monster. They screamed giddily.

"C'mon!" Paula directed the others. "Everyone, throw snowballs at the Winter Beast!"

The Winter Beast got totally pounded. Some of the snow got into the collar of my jacket, and it was ice-cold. As I continued my unholy rampage, I remember stealing a glance back at Maria. It wasn't much, but there was small smile on her lips.

For a second, I grinned back at her.

Then I saw the snow packed into her mitten.

Maria nailed me in the face. With a sharp cry, I fell into the snowy yard, and the little brats finished me off.

CHAPTER
FIFTEEN

I SEIZED A gold-tinged cocktail from the waiter's plate, then retreated into a corner of Our Leader's grand ballroom. Seeking to avoid accidental eye contact, I pretended to admire some towering drapes that resembled a faded version of the American flag.

I don't usually go to Our Leader's parties. They're these super-glamorous affairs in which a couple hundred politicians and other so-called important people pack into a room and pretend to like one another. The truth is that all these sycophants are there for themselves. They will do whatever it takes to get ahead, whether that means kissing an ass, stabbing a back—or both at the same time.

But I digress. As I was saying, I generally avoid these things. I skipped the holiday extravaganza earlier this month without much trouble. Look, it makes sense for the Communications Director and Press Secretary to go, but the Crisis Communications Manager's job is to stay in the shadows. Scott agreed when he was in charge, but now we had someone with a somewhat different perspective.

Victoria's thinking was that there could be a crisis. I protested that it was unlikely on New Year's Eve, and even if there was, the news media probably wouldn't notice. Most of the print journalists got the holiday off, while cable news liked to keep their cameras trained on the news anchors getting silly drunk. But Victoria was not convinced. This was only the second New Year's Eve with Our Leader as President, and the fact that there wasn't a crisis last year seemed to increase the chances of one this year. It was hard to disagree there.

It wasn't as if I had any better plans. Last year, I didn't get to kiss Maria at midnight because she was hosting the channel's ridiculous New Year's coverage. Confetti rained across my TV screen while my wife popped a bottle of champagne. I had toasted the image of Maria with a three-quarters drained bottle of Scotch, then passed out on the sofa.

Rather than continue staring at the drapes as if they contained the answers to the universe, I forced myself to return to the party. I spied Joe Steele chatting up Victoria. The lanky founder of Woozle had a lot of nerve coming here, given his support for Jason Stonybrook in the last election. He was wearing a crisp hoodie—Steele famously bragged that he never wore the same zipped sweatshirt twice. This hoodie was black with a silver image of clinking champagne glasses on the back. Steele's blond hair was buzzed to a fuzz, and he wore cyan glasses shaped like the digits of the coming year. He looked eighteen even though he must have been in his thirties.

He was once Joseph Stellberg, a sallow-faced nerd who lived twenty minutes from the beach but never put one foot into water. Joe started up Woozle in his dad's garage with three other similarly sun-hating geeks. The Woozlers, as they had called themselves, clacked away on laptops all senior year.

Famously, Stellberg flunked most of his spring classes

and missed his chance to be high school valedictorian. Rumors spread as to why. Drugs, guessed some, but that was quickly dismissed as it made the geek sound way too cool. An all-consuming romance? That was closer to the truth, if you could count a computer as a lover.

Woozle launched its first app, Woozler, the same day that Principal Reginald Jenkins was to meet with the Stellbergs about young Joseph's falling grades. The Stellbergs left the meeting determined to discipline their son, only to find their kid in the garage watching his bank account explode. They quickly forgot about being mad.

Woozler was a near-perfect melding of messaging, social network, augmented reality, and Gamification as a Service (GaaS), which is to say that no one really knew how to describe it. High school kids took first to Woozler, but its audience quickly expanded to their older siblings in college, and later their lame parents. While I consider myself pretty good at many elements of PR, I could never quite figure out how to maximize the value of social media. I guess that's why we had Debbie.

Eventually, Joseph Stellberg dropped out of school and legally changed his name to Joe Steele, after his avatar in the popular first-person shooter *Dark as Day*.

I saw the little nerd curl up his lips and flash his trademark buck-toothed grin at Victoria. Figuring I should make sure the former intern wasn't spilling state secrets, I crossed the floor to see what they were giggling about.

Senate Majority Leader Ed Baker intercepted me. He held a big plate, balancing two pork sliders, a shrimp-and-bacon skewer, several chunks of cheese, and a spread deck of crackers.

"Is that the Hammer?" he blurted, spraying crumbs into my face.

The senator knew me from when I was a blogger. I'd written about some particularly insensitive remarks he'd made about vegans. Baker smartly took my advice to propose a bill requiring non-meat alternatives at fast food restaurants, which they pretty much all had already. Not only did it make for a good talking point, but it got him out of the sty.

"Nice work this year keeping the President in check," he said while chewing on the skewer. "That is one crazy motherfucker."

"No sore feelings about the primary?" I asked. Our Leader had whomped him in the preliminary round of the election.

Baker licked his teeth. "So long as he keeps signing my bills, I'll be pleased as a pig in the mud. And I do mean mud."

And you do mean pig, I thought. I didn't much like the senator. Incidentally, by "bills," I'm fairly sure he meant legislation. However, I didn't put it past him to have some kind of financial arrangement with Our Leader as well.

Scott rushed up and saved me before I could say anything I might have regretted. There was an unmistakable glint of fear in his eyes as he whispered, "Need you right now in the Comms Situation Room."

Honestly, it didn't seem like much of a crisis: Our Leader was just feeling a little under the weather.

"Didn't anyone make him get a flu shot this year?" I asked, half out of jest.

Scott, taking the question seriously, replied with great remorse. "Believe me, we tried. But you know how he feels about vaccines..."

Victoria burst into the Comms Situation Room. "What's going on?"

I shrugged. "Our Leader is sick and doesn't have a voice."

"He has a voice," said Scott. "It's just that he sounds like a frog."

"Are you sure he's not just drunk?" asked our boss. "He made me bring him a bottle of bubbly pink Moscato about an hour ago, and it was clearly not his first."

Scott shook his head. "No, Our Leader can still sing when he's drunk. This is something else."

"So, what? You're saying that he can't do his New Year's song?" asked Victoria, shrugging like it didn't matter. "We'll just skip it this year."

"Skip the song?!" Scott looked mortified. "We can't *skip* it. Our Leader believes that his performance is the only reason people come to his New Year's parties. He'll say the party is a failure if he doesn't get to sing. And if he thinks that the party is a failure, he'll be really, really mad. Who do you think he'll take that out on? Rico, back me up here."

I squinted at him with concern. "Uh, Scott? Rico's not here."

Scott checked the room to confirm. "What...still?"

"Anticipation is growing for Our Leader's song on social," commented Debbie, emerging from beneath the desk. "Joe Steele is planning to do a live stream on Woozler."

Shaken by Debbie's sudden appearance, I demanded to know what she was doing under the table.

"I had to charge my phone," she answered as if it was the most obvious thing in the world. "My cord didn't reach."

"Can we please stay on topic?" snapped Victoria. "Blake, you're supposed to be the Crisis Communications Manager. What do we do?"

I was feeling skeptical about the whole thing, as it seemed to be veering into the territory of what we in the PR business call "Generating a crisis." This occurs when one tries to manage a problem that's not really a crisis and ends up enlarging the matter into a full-blown debacle. Not to be confused, by the way, with "Manufacturing a crisis," a skillful PR tactic in which one deliberately creates a fake crisis to divert attention from a real crisis. Such as, for instance, fabricating an emergency alert about an incoming missile.

"This really isn't what you're paying me for," I groused. "The hound—now that was a crisis."

"Hashtag #HeroPup!" chirped Debbie.

Scott's face had gone full red. "It's damn well going to be a crisis when Our Leader flops in front of the crowd! Who knows what he'll do? What if he makes us breathe in his flu germs?"

"Wait, you're worried he's going to stand over us and sneeze?"

Scott stuck up his arms. "Blake, you know, it would be really nice if you would stop rubbing it in that you had time to get a flu shot this year."

"You didn't get one, either?" I exclaimed incredulously. "They were free in the cafeteria!"

Victoria made a face. "I never eat there. That place is just *crawling* with germs."

"Who here got a shot this year?" I persisted, raising my hand.

"Wait," said Debbie, looking up from her phone. "Someone got shot? Should I wooze about it?"

"No!" I snapped. After a deep breath, I tried to bring the room back to order. "Look, if Our Leader doesn't have a voice, why don't we just play a recording and have him mouth the words?"

Debbie looked skeptical. "People generally don't like when singers lip-sync. That kind of thing can go viral, and not in a good way."

Scott, likely still thinking about the flu, looked completely perplexed.

"They're not going to find out," I put in before my colleague could again derail the discussion. "Our Leader's done a lot of music videos—he shouldn't have any trouble! We'll use a live version of the song, or like a demo recording without much production, so it sounds like he's doing it for real. And maybe we can project something flashy on the wall behind him, so people don't focus too closely on his mouth."

Scott pumped his fist. "The Hammer does it again!"

Victoria said without enthusiasm that it sounded fine. "Our Leader's going on a half-hour before midnight, so you've got two hours to get ready."

Our Leader looked a shade greener than usual as he lurched onto the stage five minutes late. The room exploded with applause, which was a very good thing since it looked as if the President was having some trouble catching his breath.

The President leaned into the mike as the hooting and hollering subsided. "I'm very glad, though not surprised, to see you all here at my glorious New Year's gala." His voice sounded a little hoarse, but I hoped people would blame it on the sound system. "I throw the best parties. You're welcome."

Another cheer erupted from the crown. I checked the cameras in the back and saw several sustained red lights, indicating that this was live on Triple N and other TV networks. I spotted Joe Steele holding a phone aloft to livestream the performance on Woozler.

"I've got a little—" A tiny gag cut off his sentence.

Uh-oh.

The President gazed down at his feet and held up one finger to say he needed a second. "Excuse me. I've got a little number for you about this special—" he gulped "—special day, which I think some of the fan base might recognize."

The President guzzled a neon-green soda, then pointed the bottle sharply at the deejay. "OK, hit it!"

A recording of Our Leader's hit song, "Workin' for the New Year" played over the speakers. Everyone knew this one. The chorus goes: "Work, work, work, work! Been workin' for the New Year!" About a thousand times.

Our Leader was never a graceful dancer, but he seemed especially off the beat tonight. It almost looked as if he was drunk. At least his lip-syncing was on-point. And, looking around, the crowd seemed to be into it. Of course, we had plied them with plenty of wine ahead of the performance. We could only hope the people watching this at home had been doing the same.

Standing by my side, Victoria whispered, "Are you sure this was a good idea?"

"The song is only four minutes," I replied, brushing her off.

"What are we at now?"

I bit my lip. "I don't know, maybe one minute?"

Yes, I was starting to worry, too.

The song reached the part where the background music drops out and Our Leader is supposed to operatically solo one long sustained "Oh!" Just about halfway through the note, the President grasped his stomach and projectile-vomited straight into the audience.

Most of the lemon-lime slime hit the cream dress of Education Secretary Karima Wonkers. As she squealed, it hit me that we had done exactly the thing that I had feared. From a minor problem, we had generated a crisis. And I had walked us right into it.

I saw Victoria on stage trying to help Our Leader as the song continued without him.

"Turn off the music and the stage lights!" I screamed to a nearby technician. Then, running to the still-filming television cameras, I shouted, "Show's over! Shut it down!"

Somewhere along the way, I tripped over Scott—who

I learned afterward had fainted—and went sailing into a buffet table.

My head throbbed as I came to on the steel-gray carpet of the Comms Situation Room. I'm not completely sure how I got there.

Scott, also conscious again, paced back and forth across the room. "This is bad," he kept saying. "This is bad. This is bad. This is bad."

Debbie and Victoria pored over a tablet reading Woozler.

"What are people woozing?" I asked, rising to my feet.

Debbie clicked her tongue. "They're mad about the lip-syncing. Like, *really* mad."

This took me slightly aback. "What about the vomit?"

The social media guru shrugged. "No one's really woozing about the vomit. But they're positively spewing about the lip-syncing."

She projected her phone onto one of the big TV screens to show us the top trending posts. The first was from @GodAlmighty2 and said: *Go to hell, Our Leader.* @OurLeaderFanGirl69 wrote, *ru serious? I feel so betrayed.* She added a broken heart emoji. *Perfect way to close out a shitty year.* That was from @1moodydude.

Scott was hyperventilating into a brown paper bag. I snatched it away and got him to sit down.

"Why don't we just tell them why he was lip-syncing?" Victoria asked reasonably. "The President is sick. Maybe they'll feel bad for him."

Scott's mouth contorted into an expression of pure

horror. "Our Leader doesn't like people feeling bad for him! He says it makes him seem weak. He'll feed us piece-by-piece to the hounds just to prove his strength!"

"Let's wait a little longer before we respond," I said, checking my watch. "We've got only about five minutes until midnight. Pretty soon everyone will be counting down to the New Year. They'll forget all about this and Woozler will be full of hashtagged resolutions. All we have to do is run out the clock."

Victoria looked skeptical but couldn't offer a better idea. Throwing up her arms, she left the room to rejoin the party. She claimed that it was to check the temperature but I'm sure what she really wanted was a drink. Debbie had already disappeared.

I grabbed a seat at the table with Scott and we watched Maria on TV. She was standing outside in the cold, wearing a glamorous fur coat and chitchatting with a handsome actor. Running out the clock seemed to be working, and I should have felt happy, but seeing television glass between myself and Maria damped my mood.

Scott poured me a glass of champagne and joined me to watch the countdown. "Happy New Year, Blake."

"I guess."

Right then, I made a resolution: This would be the last time I spent this holiday in the Compound.

PART
TWO

CHAPTER
SIXTEEN

MAGNANIMOUSLY, VICTORIA ALLOWED each member of our team a one-week staycation that commenced upon—and included—New Year's Day. It turned out to be more of a work-from-home arrangement, but luckily we didn't face any major crises while the President recovered his strength. Maria had the week off, too, and we managed to find a few nights to eat at our own dining table. I even got to cook a couple dinners, including hamburgers and pork chops. It was nothing elaborate but gave me a tantalizing taste of home life.

I'd wanted to start the new year off right by doing a grand gesture to show Maria how much I cared about our relationship. Al and Randy had suggested that I quit, and it was an idea I knew my wife would support. I'd definitely considered resigning, but by the time I returned to the office, the idea of walking out seemed a little extreme. I liked my job—in theory. I got to be creative dealing with Our Leader's crises, which was challenging and could be rewarding. I got paid pretty well, and it was a high-profile gig that was sure to look good on my resume...if I could make it through Our Leader's first term.

I decided to take the somewhat less daring step of asking for a vacation—a real one. Maria and I would finally go on our long-planned tropical honeymoon. I hadn't taken any time off since I took the job, and the time had accrued, so technically I had somewhere between one and two months at my disposal. The only tricky parts would be getting permission and negotiating which days in the calendar would be least inconvenient for the administration. I knew they would probably still ask me to be on call in case there was an emergency, but it would still be better than no vacation.

I was headed to Victoria's office to figure out all of this when she suddenly came sprinting down the hallway. "Blake!" she snapped. "Where have you been? I need you to do something for me immediately."

I had a jelly donut in my mouth and tried to swallow it quickly. However, when I tried to talk, I could only manage a powdery rasp.

She stopped in her tracks and considered me as if I was a dirt clod on clean kitchen tile. "Why don't you take a second to chew and try again?"

Washing down the sugar with a gulp of coffee, I did so. "Can I talk to you for a few minutes first?"

"Can it wait? With Rico in the..." She stopped her sentence with a frown. "With Rico out sick...I need you to deal with all of the press e-mails we're getting."

I was appalled. "Can't Debbie do it?"

"Debbie doesn't know how to write in whole sentences. She barely uses whole *words* when she woozes."

"What about Scott?"

Now Victoria looked appalled. I tried to explain how it was better for Our Leader if I stayed more behind the scenes, but she didn't seem to be buying that, either. "It's just that if my name's all over the place, people will start asking questions I don't want them to ask," I explained. She still looked flummoxed, so I added, "I just don't want to make things hard for Maria, you know?"

"Who?"

"Maria Worthington," I answered with gritted teeth. "You know, my wife." I'd almost forgotten how new Victoria was.

My boss's eyes protruded. "*The* Maria Worthington? Triple N's Maria Worthington?"

"Yes!"

"Married *you*?"

"What, are you against interracial couples?"

"No, I'm against inter-physiognomical couples— beautiful women procreating with fat uggos," she shot back. Modulating into a baby voice, she continued, "But it's very sweet of you to protect her, Blakey-boo."

"I'm not... Maria doesn't need any protection."

Scott, who happened to be walking by, raised his eyebrows twice and bellowed, "Whoa there! Can somebody spell T-M-I?"

Palming her face, Victoria grumbled, "I hope you can see now why I don't want that eighth-grade asshole answering e-mails."

"Oh, come on, Scott's not so bad."

She wasn't convinced. "No, it's got to be you. How about this, then? Be Rico."

"What?" I responded, taken aback. "If you're asking me to drink the milk, I am definitely not—"

"Not the milk," she snapped. Victoria took a pad of paper from her pocket and scrawled Rico's username and password. Speaking slowly, as if I were an idiot, my boss said, "Answer the e-mails as if you are Rico."

"What if someone calls?"

"Calls?" repeated the twenty-something. "We still get...calls? Like, phone calls?"

I didn't want to sound old, so I said, "Well, yeah. I mean, some of the reporters—you know, like Babs Goldstein—have been around a while..."

Victoria made a face as though she was choking on a hairball. "That old, forgotten bitch can leave a voice mail!"

Harsh.

It was only as I was trudging toward Rico's office that it occurred to me that I'd forgotten to ask Victoria about vacation. I didn't feel like running after her, so I put it off.

Rico's walls were as barren as the man's personality. Our (former?) Press Secretary had a TV on the wall, which I immediately turned to Triple N. I liked having the news on while I worked because it often provided context for reporters' questions. Sometimes, it even provided useful material I could use to send a questioner on an altogether different path.

Not having to take calls was kind of a relief, actually. When reporters call, you have to come up with spin on the fly. E-mails let you carefully plan your response.

I shook the mouse and logged onto Rico's computer. There were a bunch of e-mails to answer, but the first thing I did was open the SENT folder. If I was going to pretend to be Rico, I figured that I would need to get down his voice. I assumed this would be somewhere between bored and suicidal, but figured it was good to check.

Rico's last several messages were sent just before his disastrous press conference about Project Milkman. Answering a question by Cory Boozman from *Olde New Times Today* about what was in the milk, Rico had written: *What's up, Cory? Great weather for skiing, am I right? Anyway, going to have to decline to comment on this one. Off the record, not for attribution, this shit is even better than what came out of your mama's titties. Just kidding, dude! Nothing is that good.*

Well, that was unexpectedly unprofessional. My head throbbed at the use of profanity in official correspondence, though at least he'd kept the *shit* and *titties* off the record.

I scrolled down to another e-mail. Joan Ross from WARK radio had asked how we chose the towns for Project Milkman, and if it had anything to do with how their district voted in the last election.

Rico had responded: *Hey, Joan! How are the kids? Anyway, on background, not sure I understand your question because as you know, that district voted for Jason Stonybrook by a wide margin. If there is a Project Milkman, which there is not, it would have been an honor for those towns to be selected. So, we don't see a relationship there. Off the record, try the milk before you knock it. It's un-fucking-believable.*

It occurred to me that Rico likely was drinking the milk while composing these more recent e-mails, so it was probably incorrect for me to interpret these messages as his usual style. Scrolling back a little further to the time of the hound crisis, I found Rico's response to a hard question from Babs (she did use e-mail!) about reports of deaths in the neighborhood where the hound had attacked.

Rico replied: *No comment. Off the record, you might want to check your source on that.*

This was brilliant, actually. Not only had Rico said nothing on the record, but he had implied that Babs was incorrect without allowing her to tell readers the government was saying so. Sober Rico wasn't bad! Boring, maybe, but at least this was a style that I could emulate.

Switching back to the task at hand, I opened a new unread e-mail from Brett Banner: *Hope you're doing well. This is Brett Banner with the* Banner Bulletin. *I'm writing about the false alarm in today's bulletin. When did the government learn the alarm was false and what are you doing to make sure it doesn't happen again? Thanks, Brett Banner, The* Banner Bulletin.

Resisting the urge to tell Banner in which orifice to stick his bulletin, I crafted a ho-hum message based on the statement we had released earlier. I blamed Dr. Falz for the fiasco and claimed we had already fixed the problem—not a lie, given there was never a problem. Seeking to copy Rico's usual not-for-attribution endings, I closed with: *Off the record, it might be good background for your readers to know that Dr. Falz was hired by the previous administration.*

Always a good idea to blame your predecessors whenever possible.

Feeling pretty good about myself, I opened an e-mail from Jonathan Ito of *Politi-Go-Go*. He'd written: *Rico baby, tell me you guys are fixing the missile alarm system?*

The next time I receive a warning that your long rod is incoming, I want it to be true.

Was Jonathan Ito...flirting with Rico?

Driven more by my desire for good gossip than anything else, I searched for previous conversations with Jonathan Ito. In one message, Rico closed with a winky face, followed by *Let's have another off-the-record nightcap soon.*

Huh. I was all for building relationships with reporters, but our Press Secretary didn't seem to be keeping it professional.

Returning to Ito's more recent e-mail, I clicked REPLY and attempted to compose a response. After several attempts at a suitable reply, I went with *No comment!* and a winky-face emoji. I hoped he wouldn't have any follow-up questions.

Next up was a fresh missive from Babs. As was typical, she was following a completely different story than the other reporters.

I've checked with several people close to Joe Steele, and they are saying they haven't seen or heard from him since the New Year's party last week. Some sources are telling me that Our Leader was very angry with Steele for livestreaming his disastrous lip-syncing performance. Does the administration know anything about Steele's whereabouts? Would you like to respond to these concerns?

My throat felt dry from my jaw hanging open, so I took a swig of water. I remembered too late that I was sitting at Rico's desk and it was his half-consumed bottle that I was drinking from. Not the milk, thankfully, but it was warm and I gagged reflexively.

Babs of course seemed to be implying we had something to do with Steele disappearing. But I didn't even know that Steele had disappeared. I hadn't heard that from anybody before this e-mail. I thought about double-checking with Our Leader, but...I didn't really feel like dealing with him yet.

For now, I just wrote: *We're not going to comment, but off the record, this is the first I've heard of this, and you might want to do a little more checking to confirm he's not just home with a cold.*

Minutes later, Babs replied: *Thanks, but please remember I've been doing this for three decades. I wouldn't ask about this if I was not thorough in my checking. I will keep following this story and will follow up if I learn more. Please let me know if you decide to comment later.*

I chose not to respond to that.

I worked pretty much without distraction until Scott came banging on the door. "Blake, you in there?" he shouted.

I let him in.

"I've been looking for you everywhere!" he cried.

"Yeah, Victoria made me answer Rico's e-mails. I'm actually learning a lot."

Scott raised his eyebrows. "About the press?"

"About Rico."

Scott seemed intrigued, but quickly shook the expression off his face. "I have something to tell you first. Our Leader was *poisoned.*"

I jumped up from my chair. "Is he OK?"

"What? Yeah, he's fine. I don't mean he was poisoned

a few minutes ago. I mean he was poisoned *on New Year's Eve.*"

The full meaning of this started to soak in. "Before the party?"

Scott nodded vigorously. "It wasn't the flu, Blake. The doctor just told me. She said it was probably mixed into something he drank to hide the bitter taste. I'm thinking someone put it in one of those extra-sweet sparkling wines he was swigging. It wasn't the kind of poison that would have killed him, but whoever did it wanted him to get sick."

"But who would...?" I didn't finish the question because I realized it was a silly one. Probably a lot of people would like to get back at Our Leader for something, especially the people who worked for him.

"Do you think we should put this out there?" asked Scott. "Maybe it would help explain his embarrassing performance—put him in a more sympathetic light?"

I shook my head. "I don't think so. Everyone's moved on from that already, so there's no reason to bring it up again. Anyway, someone poisoning Our Leader and getting away with it isn't a good story for us. We wouldn't want to project weakness. Does Victoria know?"

"I didn't tell her yet. I wanted to get your take first. I made the doctor promise not to tell Our Leader, obviously. Didn't think we would want another witch hunt like what happened after that bird cracked his window and Our Leader thought it was a sniper."

A good point. Chewing on an errant fingernail, I concluded, "Better if we keep this between us."

CHAPTER
SEVENTEEN

I NEVER GOT a chance to talk to Victoria about taking a vacation, but on the plus side, I left on time! It seemed like a good opportunity to take Maria out for dinner. I could at least tell her I was planning to ask about taking time off.

I told the limo driver to hold on for a minute while I called my wife. "Just need to confirm where we're going to meet."

Maria picked up after a couple of rings and heard out my dinner offer. "That sounds nice," she said, "but I've got a team happy hour tonight, remember?"

I had not remembered. "Oh yeah! Right. Was I going with you to that?"

"No, you'd be bored. It's mostly going to be a bunch of us bitching about work."

"Oh. Well, we could do a late dinner afterward if you want."

"Maybe," said Maria, adding a long pause. "I don't know, we're going to a raw bar, and I think it's likely that our crab-fest will turn into actual crab dinner. Anyway, we've got a *lot* of complaining to do so I probably will be back late."

"Oh."

"But why don't you order food or something? Watch

basketball or catch up on some video games like you're always talking about doing?"

She wasn't wrong, but for some reason a night of takeout and blowing up aliens sounded really depressing. I told her it was a good idea, though. "So how was your day, anyway?"

Maria didn't answer, but I heard someone say something in the background. Then I heard my wife's voice, muffled, telling whoever it was that she would be right there. I couldn't help but feel jealous. For a second, I even worried she might be cheating on me.

"Sorry, Blake, Gayle wants to get going. Talk tonight?"

Of course, it was just Gayle. Obviously.

"Blake?"

"Yeah, OK. Uh, Maria?"

"Yeah?"

"I love you."

"Love you, too, Ham."

I searched the coffee table for an empty spot to wedge my latest empty bottle of craft beer. Finding none, I stuck it into a Chinese paper container of half-eaten white rice.

Late-night comic Funnyman Dan had just come on the TV, and I was disappointed to find it was another rerun. Dan had been on a break pretty much since that controversial monologue he'd done about Our Leader. I guessed the network wanted him to lay low. While the President had been condemning the comedian, he certainly had never called for him to go off the air.

My cellphone rang. I struggled to get the device out of my pocket, and so didn't have time to get a good look at the ID before swiping to accept the call.

"Hey, baby," I said, carelessly assuming it was Maria calling to let me know she was finally on her way home.

"Excuse me?" came the aged voice of a woman who was clearly not Maria. I yanked the phone from my ear and saw the name *Post* on the caller ID.

Post? It was familiar but in my drunken stupor could not place it. "Sorry, I thought you were my wife."

"This is Joelle Post," she said, collecting herself after my unfortunate gaffe. "I'm...Althea's sister."

"Althea?" I gasped. My stomach clenched, knowing something must have happened.

"Al was late for class today. A student went to their office to check and, well, the doctors say it was a heart attack."

My first thought was it couldn't have been Al. The prof went for walks every day. It was much more exercise than I ever did. "Nobody could do anything to help?"

"Al was alone when it happened. By the time the ambulance arrived, it was already too late."

"Oh. That's..." I didn't know how to complete the sentence. Sad? Awful? Unfair? It was all those things but, for some reason, I couldn't say them aloud.

"We're going to have a small funeral tomorrow morning at eleven," Joelle said. "Just family and close friends. Al wouldn't have wanted us to make a big deal."

"That sounds good." It didn't seem like the right thing to say, either. Nothing was good about this.

"I know you've got a busy job, but it would be great if..."

"I'll be there. Of course I'll be there."

"Thank you, Blake."

"Uh, sorry for your loss."

"You don't need to apologize. It's a loss for both of us."

"Sorry. I mean OK."

Joelle gave me details for the funeral, which I scribbled down on a pad. We said goodbye.

For a long time, all I could do was stare at the orange-stained takeout container that hours ago had included enough General Tso's Chicken for two.

Althea had a heart attack. I couldn't believe it.

Restless but not wanting to watch any more late-night comedy, I flicked off the TV then gathered up the bottles and boxes and brought them to the kitchen. There was still some lo mein, but I dumped the whole greasy-noodle mess into the trashcan.

It was too late to call, so I sent Victoria an e-mail explaining what had happened and why I wouldn't be coming into work the next day.

The lock clicked and my front door swung open. Maria came in tipsy and smiling, but her face fell the second she saw me. I told her what had happened.

"Oh, Blake..."

She joined me on the sofa, and I lost it as soon as her arm came around my shoulder. Maria passed me tissues and held me until I could regain my composure.

My phone beeped. It was a one-word e-mail from Victoria: *Unacceptable.*

I stared at the message with disbelief.

"What's unacceptable?" asked Maria, reading over my shoulder.

"I asked for the day off," I seethed. "Should I call her? It's late."

Maria gave a mortified nod. "You should definitely call her."

"Hi, Blake," said Victoria like a mosquito come to crash an evening picnic.

"Would you please tell me what's unacceptable about taking off for a *funeral*?"

"We need you at work tomorrow. Rico is still out, and I just have this feeling that the next crisis is going to strike."

"It's a *funeral*, Victoria!"

"Yes, so you said. But not for anyone close, right? Just your old professor. That hardly qualifies as personal time. Maybe if it was someone in your immediate family..."

"Al is more family than my parents, OK?" I was shouting. "This qualifies!"

"You're upset, so I'm going to give you a pass on your tone. Look, what time is it going to be? This funeral."

Maria, worried, started massaging my neck.

"Eleven..." I said, shaking off my wife's hand. "Why?"

"Oh, perfect!" chirped Victoria. "So maybe you could still work in the morning?"

"What?"

"Maybe come in a little early? And maybe when your thing gets out, you could—"

"No," I said firmly. "I'm not doing either of those things. I'm taking the day off. And if you have a problem with that, you can take it up with Our Leader."

I hung up the phone. Then, for good measure, I turned

off the stupid thing. What I really wanted to do was smash the device to pieces, but I'd paid good money for it and held back.

I smiled at my wife. "So, I might be fired."

Maria gave me an incredulous look. "She really wants you to *work* tomorrow?"

I shrugged. "Apparently."

She kissed my cheek. "I know Al meant a lot to you."

I put my arm around her. "Do you think, maybe, that you'd be able to come with me?"

"Me?" Maria looked taken aback. "What time?"

If it was that hard for me to get out of work, there was no chance Triple N would let Maria. "Never mind."

"No, I mean, I have my morning show, but maybe I'd be done in time?"

"It's at eleven."

She gritted her teeth. "Oh. Maybe. Hmm..."

"Don't worry about it."

"Sorry, Blake."

I got up and headed up to bed.

"Ham..."

"Hope you had a nice night," I said. It came out a little more sarcastically than intended, but I didn't apologize.

CHAPTER
EIGHTEEN

THE FUNERAL WAS tough.

It was a small church. Simple. Old. There was a line for the viewing. I didn't recognize anyone, so I just waited for my turn. Some people tried small talk.

When it was my turn to see the professor, I didn't know what to say. So, I just tapped the coffin and found a seat about halfway back.

Maria had tried but couldn't take off work. She was a fly caught in a web of guilt by her spider bosses. Was it worse to stay in the web or get your head bitten off?

Maybe not a good metaphor. The spider doesn't make the fly do any work.

The ceremony opened with the National Anthem. The new one. It didn't feel like the right song to send off the prof, but I didn't say anything.

I think Joelle Post did a eulogy. I don't remember it very well. I do remember her asking me if I wanted to say a few words.

"Uh," I said, thinking *say no, say no, say no*. "Sure."

I had to squeeze past about four people because, stupidly, I'd taken a seat in the middle of the row. I shuffled to the wooden podium at the front of the room. I got another glance at Al in the coffin and, out of nowhere, this horrible sob burst from my lips.

"Sorry," I said.

"Take your time," said Joelle, sitting in the front pew. In most ways she looked nothing like her sibling. But at this moment, the older woman's face carried Al's patient and supportive expression.

"Hi, everyone. I'm Blake. I went to National University, and...well, Al was my professor. They've been my mentor ever since. Since I found out about...about..." I couldn't say it, so I waved to the coffin. "I've been thinking about the last piece of advice Al gave me...to quit my job, basically."

A few people laughed in that slightly awkward way people do when the gloom lifts at solemn occasions.

"Al expressed regret about not having grandchildren. Not sure why the prof specified grandchildren—probably they also meant children who aren't grand. I mean, I guess all children are grand, but hopefully you all get what I'm saying."

I noticed Joelle chuckling.

"Anyway, Al didn't have any kids because, I guess, work got in the way of life. I know that feeling. I love what I do, or at least I thought I did, but lately I'm not sure it's worth all the things I've given up, if that makes sense. If it was up to my boss, I wouldn't be here today. I'd be at the office, wondering why I wasn't here with Al. Well, I came here to be with Al, and...I find myself wondering why I work over there.

"Sorry, I guess I'm rambling. I shouldn't talk so much about myself at Al's shindig."

I grimaced. Shindig? What was I thinking?

"I guess I just wanted to say that I learned a lot from

Althea Post, and the truth is that I'm still learning. Maybe we all are?"

The mourners offered some affirmative grunts.

I wasn't quite sure where to go from there in this impromptu eulogy. It would have been nice to be holding a drink. Then, at least, I could have lifted my glass to lead a toast. Plus, I would have had a drink.

"Anyway," I said, turning to the coffin, "I'm really going to miss you, Al."

I nodded to the crowd to show I was finished, then headed back in the direction of my seat. I don't remember if people clapped or anything like that. I do remember that Joelle intercepted me for a big hug.

"I think the reason that Al said grandchildren rather than children," she whispered in my ear, "was because they always thought of you as a son."

I'll be honest, that made me tear up a little. Sheesh, I guess wisdom runs in the family.

CHAPTER
NINETEEN

I SHOULD NEVER have checked my phone for work messages, but as I was walking out of the church, I decided it wouldn't harm anything to peek.

Cripes, what a mistake!

Everyone on the communications team had messaged me about something happening on the Mall. Reflexively, I pulled up Triple N on my phone.

It was one of those news stories that literally made me sit down. It was cold outside, but I found a mostly dry park bench for support.

My first thought was that Triple N was showing a trailer for a new superhero movie. Maria was still on, past her usual time slot, talking breathlessly about a man in a jetpack who had floated down from the heavens and landed in the big grassy field we know as the Mall.

"This was the scene, thirty minutes ago," she said, introducing a replay of what I'd missed. There was a crowd of tourists gathering around a tall figure in silver armor and a finned helmet. A blue visor hid his eyes and nose while leaving bare a square jaw. He looked familiar. At first, I couldn't quite place it, but suddenly it came to me—he looked almost identical to the figure on those lame jetpack stickers I liked to pee on. I hated those stupid anarchists, but up to now they had at least restrained themselves to graffiti and dark-web message boards. Now there was an actual guy in a jetpack!

Heads bobbed upward to follow the flying knight rise above the growing crowd. Stopping at a height where his feet were just below their eye-level, he held up a gloved hand and flashed a peace symbol.

The people hushed.

"I am Jetpack," he said, a microphone embedded in his helmet amplifying his low, syrupy voice. "I've come to save you from your authoritarian leader."

He held out his arms like Christ on a cross. "Democracy is dying! Our nation is descending into dystopia! The little man we call Our Leader manufactured a missile crisis to make you forget about a different crisis—his government's plan to distribute a sedative to the public via milk delivery. The milk program *was* real. I know because I filmed the terrible experiment, and I was the one who sent the evidence to the media.

"I'm afraid it gets much worse. Our Leader is behind many high-profile deaths and disappearances of his sworn enemies. What happened to the late pop star Percy Penn? What about Funnyman Dan, who hasn't been seen since he joked about Our Leader's physique? Where is Joe Steele, founder of Woozle? Why did former Vice President Antonia Daniels cut short her book tour? Has anyone seen Jason Stonybrook since he lost the election?"

Jetpack paused, presumably for dramatic effect. "If they aren't dead, I suspect you'll find many of them imprisoned in the dungeons located deep below his evil Compound."

Evil seemed a bit much, and I didn't know about any dungeons, but it got the crowd riled good. They had been hanging on Jetpack's every word, and now erupted with a frightening energy I had never seen before.

"These dishonest and despicable tactics are the product of a demented leader!" Jetpack shouted through the din. "He has gotten away with them thanks to the vile spin of a PR mastermind named Blake Ham-ner."

My lips emitted a low whimper, and not just because he'd mispronounced my name.

Displaying another peace symbol, the flying knight continued, "Do not fear. Jetpack is here to help you resist your oppressive government. No, not with violence. We can take back our country with peaceful protest!"

Perhaps noticing some people in the crowd looking over their shoulders, the cameraman zoomed out to reveal Our Leader's police in full riot gear. A robotic voice boomed over the scene, "Citizens, disperse! Disperse!"

Jetpack ignored the coming soldiers. "Rally with me here tomorrow morning, then we will march to Our Leader's Compound to call for an immediate election. If you want to return to the freedom, liberty, and democracy that our nation was founded upon, I ask you to join me in this peaceful protest!"

"Disperse or prepare to be arrested!" Brandishing nightsticks, the police marauded into the crowd. Some people began to run, while others attempted to fight back.

"Stand strong!" urged Jetpack, clicking a button on his chest. "Our Leader's days are numbered!"

With a great boom, fire shot from the revolutionary's backpack. A cheer lifted from the audience, and even some of the soldiers stopped in their tracks to watch the silver knight rocket himself into the bright sky.

I knew this was bad, but before allowing myself to chew it over, I called for a government limo. It arrived in seconds; apparently, one of our driverless vehicles had literally been hovering just around the corner from the church. I presumed this had been Victoria's doing—she couldn't give me space, even for a funeral.

I had to get back quickly because Our Leader's initial response was playing right into the revolutionary's hands. Sending in police to break up the crowd only served to make the President look more authoritarian, which was exactly Jetpack's point. It made the revolutionary's claims about the various disappearances ring true.

I couldn't allow myself to believe the claims. Our Leader is certainly no saint, but I would never work for someone who imprisoned or killed celebrities and political foes.

The feud with the late Percy Penn had been mutually beneficial, I reminded myself. Explaining how they'd made each other more famous would be no easy task, but the bottom line was that there was no rational reason for Our Leader to want him dead.

On the other hand, was Our Leader really a rational man?

I had only recently learned Joe Steele was missing, but Our Leader would have to be out of his mind to think he could make the richest man in the world disappear unnoticed.

Then again, wasn't Our Leader at least a little bit out of his mind?

As for the Funnyman Dan thing—I knew Our Leader wasn't pleased with the late-night host's monologue last month, but there was a plausible alternative explanation for Dan's recent absence from the airwaves. It was typical for him to take a couple weeks off the air at various times throughout the year. I couldn't remember if this was the time of year when he did that, but certainly that was something the PR team could figure out pretty quickly to dismiss Jetpack's claims.

Man, and I really loved that show.

The other two disappearances also carried an air of believability, which could be damaging even if the allegations weren't true. Our Leader had gone apoplectic about Vice President Daniels's book, which had painted Our Leader as, well, rather apoplectic. It was also true that Prawnmeijer's political rival, Jason Stonybrook, had disappeared from the news cycle almost overnight. But I'd always chalked that up to his disastrous defeat in the election. And I felt certain that I would have known if Our Leader had actually locked up either one of them.

Yes, I was mostly, pretty much sure there was nothing nefarious going on. The trick was to prove it. How hard could that be for a "PR mastermind" like me? That's what Jetpack had called me. While nice to be acknowledged for my skills, I hadn't liked Jetpack's tone—or that he had announced my name to the public. I liked staying behind the scenes; this level of attention was the last thing I wanted. Plus, I didn't understand why he was singling me out. Why not Victoria? What about Scott?

I realized it wasn't the first time we'd encountered the

flying knight. During our visit to Avalon, I had thought I'd seen someone on the roofs. On the ride back to the Compound, our hoagie-hoovering hovercraft pilot had claimed to see a flying man. Scott and I had thought he was nuts, but now I felt sure it had been this Jetpack. He'd followed us to the test sites, hid in the shadows, and filmed the whole thing for the media. He was a treasonous spy...but I was starting to worry the public wouldn't see it that way.

"LIES, LIES, LIES!" roared Prawnmeijer. "Get this lying, flying loser off the air immediately! Then shoot him out of the air!"

The Comms Situation Room was in pandemonium. Our Leader, usually not one to leave his Throne Room, was huffing around the room in gym shorts and a sweat-drenched T-shirt. The others were seated around the table, frantically swiping smartphones and tapping on laptop keyboards.

"This isn't live footage," Scott replied calmly, which was the right tone to take when Our Leader got like this. "Triple N keeps replaying the clip from before."

"Then call up Triple N and tell them not to show those lies ever again! It's all lies! Lies, I say!"

I groaned inwardly. "We don't control what the news—"

"Do it now! I don't ever want to see that ass-pack on TV again!"

Scott snickered. "Ass-pack." He lifted his phone, but I slapped it out of his hand before he could contact the news station. My colleague looked stunned as the device clattered across the floor.

It looked as if smoke might shoot out of Our Leader's nose. "*Blake...*"

I'd had enough of trying to maintain calm and held up my hands in protest. "We'd just be playing into his hands! He said democracy is dying! What, are we going to prove his point? Those stupid policemen on the scene almost did!"

Our Leader looked hurt. "But I love democracy. Democracy is why I'm their leader."

Victoria intercepted Our Leader with a notebook. "Uh, sir, perhaps if you could tell us which things he said were lies, it would help us to—"

He smacked the pad out of her hand. "They're *all* lies! I never imprisoned any of the people he's talking about! I didn't have anything to do with Percy's death! I've been framed! It's all lies!"

"It wouldn't matter if Triple N stopped playing the tape," said Debbie morosely. "It's all over social."

I looked left and right, up and down, but couldn't locate Debbie anywhere. Finally, I realized the voice was coming from the speakerphone. That kind of annoyed me, since it meant I could have called in, too.

Debbie continued her assessment. "People are woozing their hearts out—this thing has gone viral. The weird thing is it looks like the Woozler algorithm is favoring positive posts about Jetpack. It's almost as if they're promoting the posts, but none of them have the dollar-sign tag they usually assign to paid ads."

Victoria raised her eyebrows. "You mean it's all organic growth?"

"I mean that's the way it appears..."

"Look," I said, interrupting, "the first thing we need to do is call off the soldiers. I know we're mad, but this just looks bad. We'll get out of this the same way we get out of every other crisis."

"Dumb luck?" Victoria asked derisively.

"No," I said, pausing for effect. "With good PR."

"Meaning?"

I waved at the screen, now repeating a clip of Jetpack's speech. "It shouldn't be that hard to discredit this jet-butt. I mean, c'mon, look at that ridiculous outfit!"

"Jet-butt? That's not as funny as ass-pack," remarked Scott. "But yeah, OK. I'll write up some talking points and forward them to the allies."

I nodded approvingly. The allies were a posse of friendly talking heads who went on Triple N and other networks to defend the President. They were loyal and reliable.

Our Leader yawned. "I need to lie down. You fucking flacks have until tomorrow's march to figure this out. Or else I sic the hounds on their little protest tomorrow!"

He stormed out of the room, slamming the door behind him for added effect.

The thought of our mechanical dogs ripping through a crowd of innocent people made me shudder. Was this the moment that finally pushed the President over the edge? Had we all been in denial and Prawnmeijer was really the dystopian despot everyone had feared? Maybe the protesters were against us, but I still believed in free speech. You beat words with words, not violence. I couldn't let Our Leader loose the hounds, but I also didn't think it would be easy to convince him to hold them back. The only solution seemed to be to diffuse the threat of a march so that Our Leader wouldn't have to show an iron fist.

No one said anything for a while, as if we were worried that Prawnmeijer might have faked his big exit and was actually hiding outside the door, listening in. Our faces held varying levels of anxiety. Scott, appearing the most freaked out of all, breached the silence. "You don't think he really did it, right?"

"What, put all those guys in the dungeons?" I forced an unconvincing laugh that got serious looks from the others because Scott's question was what we were all thinking. "I mean, first of all, it's not like we actually have dungeons, right? Nobody thinks we have dungeons?"

Silence from the team.

"Actually," I said, "that would make a great talking point: 'There are no dungeons, and if there are no dungeons, there are no prisoners.' Let's get the allies saying that one right away."

"I thought Rico was in the dungeons?" asked Scott.

Victoria cackled. "Rico's not in the dungeons."

Scott looked at her suspiciously. "But there *are* dungeons?"

"Would everyone shush for a second?" snapped Debbie. "I'm sending the talking point over social right now. So, are we saying there is no dungeon, singular, or there are no dungeons, plural?"

"Say there are no *dungeons*, plural," said Victoria.

Scott's eyebrows shot up. "So, there is one dungeon?"

"You used to have my job!" Victoria protested. "You would know if there was a dungeon."

My friend's large forehead turned bright red. "I was Communications Director, not Dungeon Master!"

"Enough about dungeons!" shouted our boss, raising her arms in exasperation. "Everyone, get back to work!

Blake's talking point will do for now, but we're going to need many more. So I'm going to give you guys an hour to come up with ten better ones. Send them to me, and we'll decide together which ones aren't too dumb to use."

Victoria got up to leave, but I couldn't contain my frustration with her micromanaging any longer. "Why don't *you* come up with something for a change?"

Scott gulped audibly.

"Hashtag #awkward," squeaked Debbie.

Victoria looked stunned. "You're not serious?"

"You got lucky diffusing that hound situation!" I declared. "Ever since you *stole* Scott's job, you've contributed nothing to this team except...except...headaches! Scott has been a hot mess—"

Scott looked up. "Hey..."

"—and we all know you want to get rid of the both of us. Well, I'd like to see how well you'd do your job without us."

Victoria laughed. "You think I need either of you? You're absolutely right I want to get rid of you two morons. You're both worthless! I could come up with better spin in my sleep!"

"Oh yeah?" I goaded, gritting my teeth. "Prove it!"

Scott stammered an intervention. "Uh, maybe we should just put aside our differences and—"

"Heck no!" I yelled.

"I'd rather eat a shit sandwich!" returned Victoria.

"OK, OK!" Scott held up his hands in defeat. "Ew, you'd rather eat a shit sandwich?"

"Hashtag—" chirped Debbie, but she cut herself off. "No, wait...we can't wooze that."

"How about this?" I told my boss. "Whoever takes down Jetpack first gets to lead this team."

"Fine!" she said. "And if I do, you have to resign—immediately!"

"And if it's me or Scott, *you* have to resign!"

"Fine!" she yelled, slapping the table.

"Fine!" I shouted back, also slapping the table.

Scott, who I guess was feeling a little left out, went to slap the table, too, but the F-word he used turned more profane when his hand sank into the sharp end of a notebook's wire-ring binding. The pad popped up with his bloody hand, and the former Communications Director began to shriek.

"Hey, what's going on over there?" asked Debbie from the teleconference bridge. "Is the meeting over? Can I hang up now?"

CHAPTER
TWENTY-ONE

SCOTT AND I shuffled into the elevator, and I smacked a palm against the round button that read SB-13. We were about to go low, real low.

The car slowed much sooner than I expected, and indeed, it wasn't yet our floor. "Basement Level 5," the elevator sexily clarified.

The doors opened on one of the hounds. I nearly fainted. It was on a leash attached to a handler, as it turned out, but the first thing I saw was its sharp teeth.

"Going up?" asked the handler, an older gentleman in a paperboy cap. I couldn't help but notice his arm ended in a smooth stub.

"Down," replied Scott.

The mechanical beast hummed. Or was it a low growl?

The handler leaned back to peer at the elevator call buttons. "Oh shoot, I must have hit down," he said, taking a step back.

I tapped the CLOSE DOORS button as if my life depended on it.

Scott looked concerned. "You OK, Blake?"

I didn't breathe until the elevator had resumed its descent. "Yeah...fine."

He smirked. "Talk about biting the hand that feeds you."

"Shut up! That doesn't even make sense."

When the elevator rumbled disconcertingly after Sub-Basement Level 10, Scott remarked: "You know, we're probably far enough down now that, if someone were to cut the cable, we'd survive the fall."

"Yes," I said, "and be stuck near the earth's core for the rest of our days."

The elevator wailed mournfully...then beeped pleasantly. "Sub-Basement Level 13," it chirped. The doors slid open, inviting a gust of wind that tasted old and earthy. Holding our arms to our faces, Scott and I pushed through the thick wind and out of the metal chamber.

Ironically, this cave-like environment was home to Project Overseer, a government surveillance operation. About one hundred men and women inhabited this dimly lit recess of the Compound, spending their days staring at screens of the outside world and reporting suspicious sights to the police aboveground. We had surveillance cameras attached to utility poles, light fixtures, and buildings, with a swarm of bee-sized drones to bring us views into everywhere else.

"Greetings, above-worlders," said a woman with a powder-white face who had seemed to materialize from thin air. I was 95 percent certain she was wearing makeup. I checked for fangs but couldn't find any. She looked about Scott's age, but you never could tell with vampires.

"Chief Overseer Melanie Copps?" asked Scott officially.

"Call me Mel," she said, looking him over as though he might make a good snack.

This was the first time we'd met. I'd never had much reason to come down here, and I'd never seen the Chief

Overseer aboveground. Legend had it that she hadn't seen daylight for nearly a decade.

"We're from Communications. I'm Blake, this is Scott..."

He was ogling Copps with a kind of sexual wonder. I elbowed him hard in the arm to get him to stop.

"Good morning," said Scott.

"Morning?" She seemed surprised. "Oh yes, that would explain all the sunlight we're seeing on the consoles. Well then, what brings you fine men downstairs?"

Scott seemed tickled by the phrasing but didn't answer the question.

"Jetpack," I said. "You saw him on the screens?"

Copps cackled as if the question was ridiculous. "We see all."

I gulped. "Right. Well, uh, that's good, I guess. So, anyway, we want to know where the heck he came from, where the heck he went, and who the heck he is under that mask."

"Oh heck!" she mocked, putting on a slack-jawed hillbilly accent. "We wanna know who the heck he is!"

Scott snorted. "You do say *heck* a lot, Hamner."

I gave him a sharp look. "There's a reason, you know. If you get too much in the habit of saying hell or another curse—"

"Hell isn't a curse, it's a place," interrupted Mel. "A very real place."

Scott's face darkened. "Don't I know it."

I was starting to get annoyed. "Look, are you going to help us or not?"

"Not," she said. "We don't have the information you're looking for."

Scott asked me, "Is she trying to use the Force on us?"

Ignoring him, I complained, "I thought you said you see *all*!"

Mel sighed patronizingly. "Come with me." She led us down the corridor into the main work room, an open-style office with rows and rows of screens. There was no chatter, but rather a persistent tapping of keyboards. The Chief Overseer took us to her corner office, which had a sign on the door that read DANGER! HIGH VOLTAGE!

The first thing I noticed inside was a translucent piece of plastic covering the overhead fluorescent light. It gave the effect of a blue sky with puffy white clouds and a single pink kite, and yet somehow reinforced the fact that we were miles underground. As Mel sat behind her desk, I noticed Scott studying a framed photo of the Chief Overseer lying on the beach in a bikini. I wondered when she had managed to take a vacation. I imagined the caption would say something like, *Shot one hour before the worst sunburn of Mel's life. She's never been outside since!*

Mel spun around her monitor so we could see.

"This is an aerial view of the Mall, as photographed by one of our bee drones," she said. "That's Jetpack in the middle, finishing up his speech. Now watch, as he takes off into the air."

Jetpack grew larger on the screen as he got close to the camera, then shifted off screen. The drone followed for a few seconds, but then something weird happened. Jetpack seemed to vanish into thin air.

"Where did he go?" cried Scott.

Copps shrugged. "We checked CCTV footage before he appeared and it's the same thing. He seems to just materialize out of thin air."

"Could he have been some kind of projected holo-gram the whole time?" asked Scott.

The Chief Overseer scrunched her eyebrows. "A good thought, but no. We think he's got tech in the suit that makes him invisible to the cameras."

I could feel a headache coming on. "A surveillance shield? That's a thing?"

She leaned back in her chair. "Why not?"

This wasn't going to be as easy as I thought. "Well, could you figure out anything about his identity when he was on camera?"

"Negative. The visor covers just enough of his face to prevent facial recognition, and he's using tech to disguise his voice."

"Cripes!"

Scott punched my shoulder. "Just curse already, Hamner!" He chuckled idiotically, then cleared his throat. "Hey, Copps, may I ask you something?"

She smiled. "I said you can call me Mel."

"Mel, then," he repeated, seemingly pleased by the sound coming out of his mouth.

"Yes?"

He pointed to the bikini picture. "When's the last time you've been—?"

"Out?" she replied quickly.

"To the beach."

The pale lady licked her top incisors. "Why? Would you like to take me?"

Scott wanted to keep flirting, so I got the heck out of there.

The elevator shuddered violently between Basement Levels 4 and 5, but I survived the trip to the surface. I went straight to the courtyard for a deep breath of fresh air. The sun felt great.

My cellphone jolted me from my meditation, beeping incessantly with all the notifications I'd missed while underground. A couple of texts were from Maria. Turned out Victoria was going to come on TV to talk about Jetpack. She'd demanded that my wife do the interview, even though the afternoon wasn't her usual time slot.

Subjecting myself to an interview by a journalist as good as Maria most definitely would not be my play at this point, with our backs already against the wall. I thought about calling Victoria to tell her not to do it. But then I thought if she wants to throw herself under the bus, who am I to stop her?

I returned to my office to think. When that didn't work, I poured myself something to drink. I didn't feel like getting any ice, so it was a whiskey straight, and a fairly tall glass at that.

I thought it might help to think about what I would have recommended if I was still an outsider with a crisis-PR blog. Happily, giving myself a little distance from my job gave me the inspiration I was seeking. The right approach, I realized, was honesty. We could invite Triple N and other reporters with their cameras into the Compound and let them see for themselves that we hadn't locked up the missing people here. They would see we didn't have any dungeons.

Doubts crept in like the spindly legs of a centipede. I'd been off my game lately. My gussied-up hound had nearly been the death of me. My way out of the Project Milkman crisis could have wrecked my marriage. On top of all that, I kept thinking about Althea and how the last advice they'd given me before they died was to do something else with my life.

A voice in my head told me transparency would never work anyway. Even if Our Leader agreed to letting reporters into the Compound—pretty unlikely given how much he valued his privacy—there was no way the President would ever give reporters *full* access. Whatever rooms we kept locked would become the dungeons in the media's eyes.

And maybe we did have dungeons! I couldn't say for sure.

Approximately halfway through my second glass of whiskey, it seemed like a wise idea to retrieve the Grand List of Distractions from the Comms Situation Room.

Sitting at the empty roundtable, I ran a yellow highlighter carefully over each line item, giggling a little here and there.

"Got one in mind?" asked Scott, slipping into the room. He had blood-red lipstick on his cheek and one side of his collar was flipped up.

"What happened to you?" I asked. "Wait, don't answer that."

Scott grinned broadly, and I must say I'd never seen him so relaxed. "Let's just say I was...overseen quite well."

Ignoring the lame double entendre, I pointed to the

list. "So, I don't have one idea in mind. I've got several." I explained that we would flood the airwaves with many minor crises at once. The almost biblical amount of crazy nonsense would generate enough questions to keep the media occupied for days. It would divert people's attention into so many stressful directions that their only choice would be to pull inward and shut out the world completely. "They'll wish they were in a cave with their fingers in their ears!"

Scott shrugged. "OK, where do we start?"

I took a swig of my drink. "Honestly? I think I can knock off a lot of these in a single speech."

He slapped me hard on the back. "Hah! That's why they call you the Hammer!" Reading the list over my shoulder, he asked, "Hey, how come you didn't highlight the one about the zoo?"

I furrowed my brow "Oh, I just don't really know how I'd make that work in a speech, you know?"

"No," said Scott with a furtive smile, "but we could just do it now, anyway."

I wasn't sure. It also sounded kind of dangerous. The plan could go horribly wrong in a multitude of ways. I don't think I would have even considered it had I not been drinking.

"C'mon, please?" wheedled Scott. "You know I came up with that one. I'm feeling a little insulted it's the only one you're not doing."

I drained the rest of my whiskey and placed the glass on top of the Grand List's existing brown stain. It seemed to me it might be good to give Scott something to do while I tried to write Prawnmeijer's speech.

"Please, please, please? It will be so good, Blake. You're a smart guy. You know it will work."

"Fine," I said at last, pushing him out of my personal space with a wave of my hands. "Call the National Zoo. Tell them to release the animals."

CHAPTER
TWENTY-TWO

A BURLY RHINO exploded into a snacks booth, blasting popcorn and peanuts in all directions. An elephant stampeded in and went straight for the peanuts. Above, a monkey shrieked triumphantly. It was stupid, reckless, and I never should have allowed it.

Shaking my head, I put the chaos on mute, and returned to writing my speech. It was going to be one of the worst speeches I'd ever written, but that was intentional, so in a way it was going to be one of the best speeches I'd ever written. I was actually having a lot of fun. It's quite freeing to put aside all the seriousness and just cut loose occasionally.

I got a bunch of texts from Victoria and Debbie that I didn't read. Forty-five minutes flew by. I didn't look away from my PC screen until Scott burst into the room, looking as if he'd just narrowly escaped a flamethrower.

"Why did you let me do that?!" he screamed. "Our Leader is pissed!"

I blinked. "What, he doesn't like zoo animals?"

"Haven't you been watching?" yelled my colleague, gesturing frantically toward the TV.

I gaped at the image on the screen. Jetpack was standing in front of the lion's cage, and *the lion was in the cage*. A starry-eyed young woman had a microphone in the jerk's face.

I looked at Scott. "Wait, you mean he—?"

"Yes."

"All of the—?"

"All."

"By him—?"

"By himself."

The knight placed his hands triumphantly against his hips. I grabbed the remote and turned the sound back on just in time to hear Jetpack declare, "All in a day's work!"

"So, what, they're calling him a—?"

"A hero to the people!" burst the blushing reporter.

Jetpack brushed aside the compliment with a flick of his wrist. "Oh no, I'm just doing what's right."

"Jetpack, how do you think the animals got out?"

Dropping his arms back to his sides, the super-idiot's expression turned grave. "Well, Dana, I do have an idea about that. You see, I spoke to the zookeeper, and he informed me that he was ordered by the government to let the animals loose."

The reporter gasped. "But why would they do that?"

"Seems like this is just another example of the government trying to distract the people from the truth that we are ruled by an authoritarian dictator. This must end, but I can't save us alone."

He stuck his blue visor in the camera, breaking the fourth wall.

"If you're with me, please join me in protest tomorrow at the National Mall."

I banged my head against the keyboard. "No, no, no, no!"

"What's up, guys?" asked Debbie, springing up behind me.

"Jetpack's dick," responded Scott. "And it's got our butts in the crosshairs."

The Social Media Director looked disgusted. "Uh, hashtag #gross. Well, I may have *some* good news. The Hero Pup naming contest—"

"Are you serious, Debbie?!" I screamed, rising from my chair in fury. "Can't you see we have more important things to worry about?"

The social guru gave me the side-eye. "OK, whatever, I'll come back later..."

I offered my most encouraging nod.

Maria appeared on screen in a fetching orange pantsuit. "Welcome to *Your News Today*. I'm Maria Worthington. Hours ago, we met the mysterious Jetpack when he landed in the Mall and boldly called for revolution against Our Leader! Then, just minutes before this broadcast, we saw Jetpack single-handedly avert potential disaster when several large animals escaped the National Zoo. Jetpack has claimed that Our Leader ordered the zoo break as an intentional distraction, all to avoid a direct response to Jetpack's calls for new leadership. Luckily for us, we have someone from the government with us right now to respond. Back with us again is Our Leader's new Communications Director, Victoria Chu."

"Here we go," said Scott with a smirk. "Let's see what she's got."

It didn't surprise either of us that Victoria would go on TV again. It seemed like the only play she had in her book. Last time had been pretty disastrous, so I wasn't worried she'd win our little game with this gambit.

Anyway, she couldn't have been prepared to answer for our zoo stunt.

To my delight, Victoria looked positively rattled when she appeared on-screen. "I, uh, I just want to say up front that I don't know anything about what happened at the zoo."

The news anchor leaned in. "You mean that you don't know if Our Leader ordered the zoo break as a distraction?"

Victoria shook her head. "I mean that I'm sure Our Leader didn't know anything about it."

Actually, that was a pretty good answer, because what Victoria said was entirely true. We had, after all, acted completely unilaterally on this one. It's bad to lie, but providing a misleading truth can be one of a PR flack's best tools.

"Anyway," continued Victoria with a barely concealed grin, "why would we create an opportunity for that jetpack-wearing weirdo to look good? That would be completely idiotic public relations. Only an utter moron would come up with something like that."

Scott looked hurt, but she was right, and I was the bigger moron for allowing it to happen.

"Well, I have to agree with you there," said Maria in a way that made me wonder if she suspected I was involved. "But let's talk for a minute about Jetpack. He made some pretty strong allegations that Our Leader is involved with the apparent disappearances of several prominent individuals."

Victoria laughed it off. "I know. So ridiculous, right?"

"You tell me."

"Maria, please. Percy Penn died a long time ago. Even the conspiracy kooks dropped that one."

I had to tip my hat to Victoria for using the long-time-ago defense. This old gem—no pun intended—was fairly simple. One implied that things that happened a long time ago were no longer fair game for discussion because they'd already been thoroughly litigated.

"Fine, but what about the more recent disappearances like Joe Steele, Jason Stonybrook, Antonia Daniels or late-night host Dan—?"

"Let me stop you there. You said yourself these are unfounded allegations."

"No, I said they're allegations—"

"Percy Penn? Seriously? That was such a long time ago, Maria."

More good spin: Keep the focus on the least tenable accusation to avoid responding to the stronger ones. However, good journalists know the best way to fight back is to persist.

"But what about the others? Where are the others?"

"Who knows? I sure don't."

"Jetpack says they're in Our Leader's dungeons."

"Maria, there are no dungeons. If there are no dungeons, there are no disappearances."

Scott flushed red. "She stole your line!"

"Actually, my bulletproof line was, 'If there are no dungeons, there are no prisoners.' Maria's about to shoot a big, fat hole in what she just said."

"Yeah, but hers has alliteration."

"Watch."

As predicted, Maria moved in for the kill. "But they *have* disappeared."

"How do you know? Did you check?"

"Triple N has independently verified that all the people named by Jetpack have not been seen for days, in some cases weeks."

"Oh, you verified, did you? And who, pray tell, verifies Triple N?"

The journalist looked ready to throttle the government spokesperson, but Maria took her small victory and held back. "Why don't we move onto something else. Tell me what Our Leader's reaction was when he saw Jetpack on TV for the first time?"

The PR rep snickered. "I don't think he gave it much notice, really. Clearly, he's a lunatic."

"Who? Our Leader?"

"I was talking about this Jetpack, obviously," sneered Victoria. "Though frankly, I'm not surprised the vindictive media would try to twist my words."

"You're saying that Our Leader didn't react at all? Excuse me, but I find that a little hard to believe given the way he usually responds to—"

"As I said, he is a lunatic. Jetpack, I mean. Jetpack is a lunatic. You don't give attention to lunatics because lunatics feed off the attention. And I think the larger public feels the same way about the whole thing."

Maria raised an eyebrow to devastating effect. "The audience at the Mall sounded pretty fired up to me. You're not worried at all—?"

"Well, the silent majority doesn't buy it. Why would anyone be worried about a clown wearing a jetpack? Who wears jetpacks? I don't think that's even legal. You should be asking if he has a license to bumble around in that thing. I don't even know why we're talking about what's-his-name."

Maria looked gobsmacked. "We're talking about Jetpack, Victoria, because you came to us and said you wanted to talk about him."

"No! That's not why I'm here. I came to tell you Our Leader is strong and carrying on! And your viewers would be well-advised to do the same!"

"Your job is to be Our Leader's mouthpiece," said Maria as levelly as she could manage. "The way you're talking says to me that he's pretty well worked up about this."

The Communications Director jumped out of her seat.

"I am not worked up! Our Leader is not worked up! This man is a lunatic! A freaking lunatic!"

"Who?" asked Maria with a wry wink at her viewers. "Our Leader?"

We laughed so loud, we had to turn up the volume to hear the rest of the interview. Victoria had started out OK, but now the interview was going off the rails. It looked as though Scott and I were going to win the bet.

Scott imitated an explosion with his hands. "Boom shakalaka!"

I wiped the tears from my eyes. "What an amateur!"

I shouldn't have counted my chickens before they hatched.

"Let me ask *you* something, Maria," Victoria said suddenly. "Why are you glossing over the fact that Jetpack also called out one of my staff as Our Leader's PR mastermind?"

Triple N's news anchor looked taken back.

"I..."

"You're not talking at all about how Jetpack called out Blake Ham-ner as a PR mastermind."

"The *n* is silent. You pronounce it like a hammer."

The President's Communications Director had the calculating eyes of a murder hornet. "Oh, that's right, I guess you would know...being his wife! Funny how you haven't mentioned that this whole time. Or maybe it's not so funny. It is kind of a conflict of interest, yes? Really takes away from your credibility as a journalist, doesn't it?"

I couldn't believe it! She was using "Attack, attack, attack." I hadn't seen this coming at all. Scott gave me a look of concern.

"Wait," replied Maria, who had clearly been caught off-guard. "You're saying that, because I'm married to Blake..."

"Now you admit it!"

"That, because I'm married to Blake, who works for Our Leader, I'm not credible when I ask the government a hard question?"

"Exactly! I rest my case."

"But, if I had a conflict, wouldn't I be asking easy questions? If anything, shouldn't I be helping Blake?"

Oh no. She shouldn't have said that.

Victoria screwed up her face and held her hands up in the air as if she couldn't take anymore. "Why does Triple N even allow you on the air? How can your viewers ever truly know if you're serving them with fair and balanced reporting?"

Maria slapped the table. "This is my show, so I think that's about enough of this interview. And you know what, *Veronica*? Don't expect to be back here anytime soon."

"Oh, I'm sure I won't be on *your* show ever again. That is, if you even have one."

Later that day, Maria would call—mad as heck—to say that Triple N had fired her.

TWENTY-THREE

Actually, I learned that Maria had been fired from a voice mail, which I didn't listen to until much later. I hadn't picked up when she called because I was too busy getting Our Leader ready to go on the air to read my "Grand Speech of Distractions."

We decided to do it in the Throne Room. Usually, we shot presidential addresses in the Rose Garden to soften Our Leader's acerbic je ne sais quoi. But for this speech, I knew that I wanted to amplify the man's craziness, so a kingly setting seemed like a natural fit.

I spotted Rico vacuuming cornbread crumbs from the large indigo cushions of the President's gilded seat. The Press Secretary was wearing dark shades indoors and didn't seem very talkative. Our Leader impatiently tapped a gold-slippered foot as he inspected the cleaning. He wore a violet blazer over a crisp white turtleneck.

I was about to approach the kid to find out where he'd been, but without warning Rico doubled over and groaned miserably. "Think I'm...think I'm gonna vom again."

"Guards!" cried Our Leader.

A pair of robed men arrived on the scene and hustled Rico out of the room.

I decided to give the speech I'd written one last read

through. I must have been sobering up, because all at once I realized what I had written was complete trash. Even if it managed to get us out of the current crisis, it was likely to get us embroiled in countless more.

Scott burst into the room looking completely flustered. I noticed a hickey on his neck but didn't have to ask to know it was from that vampire, Mel Copps. He ran up to Our Leader waving a velvet top hat, which I also might have found weird except for the fact that I'd asked him to bring it. "Sir, you've got to wear this for the speech."

The President gave him a cold look. "I don't want to wear the hat," he sneered. "It makes my scalp sweat."

"It's an important prop for the speech."

Prawnmeijer stared blankly.

"Didn't you…?"

"Too long; didn't read," Our Leader replied nasally.

Scott shouldn't have asked. Our Leader never read speeches before delivery. Sometimes he didn't read from the script while delivering it.

The President rolled his eyes and took the headpiece. "Fine…" He put it on and fell into his throne with a long groan. "Let's get this over with, please? I'm halfway through Season Three of *Halfway Across the Galaxy*, and half the crew might be dead."

Suddenly shaking, I took Scott aside. "Hey, maybe we should just cancel this whole thing? I'll go write a new speech."

Scott gave me a look. "Are you all right, Blake?"

"It's just… I think I might have had a little too much to drink when I was working on this. Plus, you know, since that hound thing? I really haven't been myself. Not to mention Althea. That whole thing just—"

"Wait, who?"

I gritted my teeth. "My mentor who just passed away. I went to their funeral, remember?"

He snapped his fingers. "Right, sorry."

"Anyway, I just reread the speech I wrote, and it's really not, um...up to my standards, you know?"

He shrugged. "I read it and it looked fine to me."

"Yeah, well, coming from you, that's not really a ringing endorsement."

"Hey, what do you—?"

The cameraman shushed loudly. When I looked up, Our Leader was live on TV.

"Salutations, my most loyal citizens," Our Leader read from the screen. "It has been some time since my last official address, but today I have several matters to discuss with you. Matters of grave importance! To begin with, I know many of you were my fans long before I became your president... Yes, I'm talking about my...singing days? It seemed to me that lately I've been neglecting my...singing?"

One of the big downsides to Our Leader sight-reading speeches was all the pauses and question marks.

"Lately," he continued tentatively, "I've been neglecting my...music. So, I hereby announce tonight a national...a national music contest? Best of all, I will be...judging? I will be judging. During the contest, all citizens must wear..." he squinted at the teleprompter "...classy hats in public."

"Men must wear top hats," he said, then pointed to his head. "Like this one, for example. Yours won't be as nice, of course. Women must wear those horse-racing hats. You know the ones I mean."

I'd meant to figure out what they called those hats but had ran out of time and left in this placeholder.

"If you don't wear a hat—or, if you wear a hat that is nicer than my hat—you will be arrested. I will announce the winner of the singing competition at our first annual...Bacon Festival? At which all attendees will receive...free bacon? The person with the best hat—myself excluded—will win a lifetime supply of bacon. But if your hat is deemed nicer than my hat, you will be tortured. Attendance at the Bacon Festival is mandatory if you live within an hour away, as measured by Woozle Maps.

"The world will be watching. No, I don't mean like how the French president hacked into my webcam last month. Ha-ha."

Our Leader looked away from the camera and sent me a quizzical stare. I gave a wide-eyed nod in the affirmative. Accusing a longtime ally of a crime was going to be a big-time distraction.

Going off script, Our Leader squealed, "That conniving bitch! Does she want war?!"

Composing himself, the President resumed reading from the prompter. "The world will be watching not just for the music contest, not just for the hats, and not just for the bacon. No, they will be watching to find out the details of my upcoming...wedding? Yes, you heard that right! I'm getting...married. I plan to announce the name of the lucky lady who will be required to marry me at the Bacon Festival. She will be the one with the best horse-racing hat. Afterward, I plan to pick the name of a tropical island from my top hat, bomb it, then honeymoon upon the remains of the dead."

Interesting how there were no pauses or question marks in Our Leader's reading of that last line.

"In closing, I'd like to leave all of you with a warning. Please do not eat any chicken for the next few months while we sort out a small issue with E. coli. Just kidding, it's actually a very big issue!"

Our Leader laughed maniacally, which also wasn't in the script, but added a nice moment of insanity before he closed. "Toodle-oo!"

Everyone in the room kept deathly silent long after we cut the feed.

"Wow," commented Our Leader. "I sounded crazy. Did I sound crazy? I think I sounded crazy."

"I think you sounded presidential," Scott reassured him.

Prawnmeijer shrugged. "Whatever. OK, everybody out! I've got a TV show to watch."

I left the Throne Room feeling a little shell-shocked. Well, maybe the speech wasn't as smart and nuanced as I would have liked, but I thought it could still maybe serve its purpose.

"That's weird," said Scott, swiping through his phone. "Not one news alert about the speech yet. Maybe the reporters don't know where to start!"

I checked my phone to confirm. No alerts, but I had a voice mail from Maria.

"But the network *knew* we were married," I insisted with a sharp whisper into the phone. "Why didn't this ever come up before?"

Maria's voice sounded huskier, as if she'd been chain-smoking e-cigarettes. "It did come up before, Blake. I told you about this. My new Woozle bosses were only keeping me on because I had good ratings. Victoria bringing it up live on TV just gave them an excuse to force me out."

"Cripes. I'm sorry, honey."

"You should know it's going to be a segment later tonight."

"What is?"

"Blake Hamner: Secret PR mastermind for Our Leader!" She said it in a deep newspaper man voice. "Or something like that. They're going to have the usual panel of pundits talking about it. They'll probably smear me, too."

"Why didn't anyone ask me for comment?"

"I think Victoria declined for you."

That was about the stupidest thing that the Communications Director could have done. Now I sounded as if I had something to hide. What I would have done is give a statement that said absolutely nothing. Then it would seem as though I was cooperating.

I must have grumbled aloud, because Maria asked, "Do you want to comment?"

I was starting to feel overwhelmed. "I mean, not live, but what if I gave a short statement? Are you still in the studio? Can you put me on with someone?"

"I went to the café in the lobby to cool off, but I haven't packed my things yet. I'll bring you up now and hand the phone to the reporter working the story."

"OK, thanks. Man, a whole segment on just me? I would have thought you'd all have enough prime-time material to chew on with the speech Our Leader just gave."

"What speech?"

I felt my breath becoming short. The Throne Room seemed to swirl around me. "Uh, the one he just delivered on live TV?"

"I don't think we covered it. Did you give us a heads-up?"

"What are you talking about? Whenever Our Leader speaks, you cover it live! Then, when it ends, you spend hours talking about it with your panel of morons. That's how it works. That's how it's always worked!"

The line seemed to go dead for a few seconds. "Why are you yelling at me? Jesus, Blake, take a breath."

I closed my eyes in shame. "Sorry. I know. You just got fired. I'm just under a lot of pressure right now."

"Well, I don't know if we would have covered it, anyway. We had Jetpack on."

"What?!"

She sighed. "I guess it was my final interview. He was kind of an interesting guy, in a mysterious masked avenger kind of way. I didn't get a good look at his face, but I kind of felt as though there was something familiar about him, you know? Like, I might have interviewed him before? There was something about his mannerisms, and the way he spoke. Just got this deja—"

I stopped listening at this point because all I could think about was what an idiot I was. Good PR reps keep an eye on the news because that context can inform how to time and angle one's message. I forgot to make sure there was nothing else on the air that would take priority over Our Leader's speech. What was happening to me?

Scott nudged me. "Hey, Blake, I just got a message from Debbie. She says everybody's woozing about a Triple N interview with Jetpack. She says 'Jetpack Savior' is trending. So is 'Not My Leader.' I don't really get why that one is bad, though. It's good they don't think Jetpack is their leader, right?"

My heart sank. "I think they're talking about Our Leader."

"Then shouldn't it be Not Our Leader? Which, technically, would apply to Jetpack."

"Scott, please shut up for a minute while I think."

"Blake," Maria put in. I'd forgotten she was still on the line. "Look, if Our Leader gave a speech, I'm sure we got the recording. They're probably editing it into a package as we speak."

"A *package*?!" I felt bile gathering in the back of my throat. A package was bad. A package could sink us.

"Hey, maybe you'll get lucky and they'll bump the PR mastermind segment. Speaking of which, I've got Caitlin with me here to take your statement. I'm giving her the phone..."

A package! I didn't have time to give Caitlin a statement. I hung up the phone and screamed, "Go to hell, you cable TV network shit-eaters!"

Meekly, a female voice from my phone responded, "OK, thanks for that... Anything you want to add?"

In horror, I checked the screen. Somehow, I'd missed the red button to end the call. I had, in fact, turned on the speakerphone.

Scott looked at me in confusion. "That doesn't sound like Maria."

"No," my voice rasped. "That's Caitlin, the Triple N reporter taking my comment."

"So much for the non-cursing rule," Scott murmured with a smirk. "Don't worry, I got this. Hey, Caitlin? Everything Blake just said was off the record, OK? We're declining comment."

Scott then took the phone from me and ended the call himself. Dusting his hands, he asked, "Jeez, Hamner, why do you still look so worried?"

Despondent, I replied, "The media doesn't have to honor 'off the record' if you fail to say it in advance."

TWENTY-FOUR

O NE OF THE big advantages of broadcasting a speech live is that it forces the media to show the whole thing uninterrupted, front to back. Even if they try to show pieces out of context later, we can point back to the original tape as a kind of holy grail. Our Leader's broadcast never appeared live, so what we'd effectively done is delegated power to the media to frame the first airing of Our Leader's speech however they wanted. As far as the public was concerned, the first broadcast of the speech would be the media package.

It was worse than expected. Triple N had interspersed their Jetpack interview with Our Leader's speech. I had intended to overwhelm people—create an experience so alarming for so many different reasons that it would frighten them back into their blissful suburban caves. But with Jetpack's cool logic as counterpoint, the President's speech merely served to underline the flying knight's reasons for rebellion.

It began with a shot of Jetpack leaning forward in his seat. "Our Leader is an unhinged, mentally unbalanced dictator," he asserted.

Then, the President: "The person with the best hat— myself excluded—will win a lifetime supply of bacon.

But if your hat is deemed nicer than my hat, you will be tortured."

Back to Jetpack: "His eccentricities may seem innocent now, but one day could lead to war."

"The French president hacked into my webcam last month," declared Our Leader, with the camera zooming in on his crazy eyes. "That conniving bitch! Does she want war?!" The package skipped ahead. "I'm going to choose the name of a tropical island out of my top hat, bomb it, and honeymoon upon the remains of the dead."

The country's would-be savior knight concluded, "We must remove Our Leader from power before it's too late."

The broadcast returned to Jake Suavo, who Maria had once told me was even more of an airhead in real life than on TV. "Coming up on Triple N: Jetpack hints he will soon reveal more evidence that Our Leader is behind the disappearances of several of his political rivals. But first! Blake Ham-ner, PR mastermind? We'll have a conversation about the President's fixer, who sounded none too pleased about our planned segment."

A recording of my voice played, with accompanying text for those who couldn't make out the scratchy telephone audio. "Go to hell, you cable TV network——!" The program bleeped out the profanity.

"That was pure propaganda!" I squealed into my phone. "And everyone keeps pronouncing my last name wrong!"

"That's your big concern?" Maria replied mockingly. She was driving home from the place she used to call work. I could tell because her voice sounded distant, like it did when she had me on speaker.

"You've got to fix this for me, Maria."

She met the demand with silence that lasted an eternity. Finally, she replied, "*Excuse* me?"

"I know you just lost your job, but the other anchors didn't decide that. You can still call in a favor, can't you? I just think that if Triple N were to play Our Leader's entire speech, uncut, it would be a little more honest than this dumb news package."

"Are you seriously asking me right now to try to influence how we report on your boss?"

I covered my mouth, realizing what I had done.

"Blake, don't you understand that this is the *exact reason* they fired me?"

I'd broken our rule not to use our marriage as leverage to get better media coverage.

"Baby, I'm sorry, I didn't mean to—"

"Never once have I demanded information about your job. I'd love to know what you do every day, Blake, and not just because it would make a good news story. Married people are supposed to share everything with each other, but you tell me barely anything about your work. I feel like I don't even really know you anymore."

"We had to make the rule—"

"You mean the one that you just broke? When we have a child—if we ever have one—are you going to lie to them, too?"

"I never lied to you, Maria."

"No, you're right, you lie to the public. You just don't tell me when you're lying to them."

That was a punch to the gut. I felt like I couldn't breathe, let alone respond.

"Look, I just got back to the house," she said. "It's been a hard day, and I need some time to clear my head. We can talk when you get home."

"OK," I said, "but about that, I'm a little worried I might have to work late tonight."

She groaned.

"It's just—there's a lot to clean up right now. I'll try to work quickly, but it's...well, it's going to take time."

"OK, Blake, if that's how you want to spend your night, I guess I'll have to be a good wife and be fine with that."

"Maria..." I pleaded.

No response.

"Maria?"

I checked my phone. She'd hung up on me.

I really deserved it, though.

"Everything OK?" asked Scott.

I shook my head. "I think I need to go home."

"Home?" he said as if he'd never heard of it before. My work colleague then wailed, "You can't go home! We're in crisis mode here, Hamner!"

I held out my hands helplessly. "So is my marriage, and I think that maybe it's more important than this job."

Scott stuck a finger in his mouth and made a gagging sound. "Not today it isn't! Blake, you can't fucking abandon me right now. Didn't you hear that Triple N douchebag? Jetpack's going to release more so-called evidence about the disappearances!"

I shrugged. "I'm useless to you, Scott. I've completely lost the knack for this work. Maybe Victoria will figure something out. She wants me out of this job? Fine, I'm out!"

I strode straight for the Communications Director's office. Victoria was back from Triple N, looking as satisfied as a black widow spider after fornicating with and then devouring her mate.

"Ready to give up?" said my boss, licking her lips.

I pointed out that she hadn't solved the crisis, either. "But yes, I'm here to resign."

She laughed. "Good one."

"I'm serious!"

The big grin lingered, though it looked as though some doubt had crept in. "Blake, you can't leave. Not now. This is a crisis. You're our Crisis Communications Manager."

"Right, your 'PR mastermind,' isn't it? And yet you're the one who seems to think you can handle things without me!" As I swung out my right arm to emphasize the point, my hand hit Victoria's potted peace lily and it crashed to the floor. Dirty water sloshed out onto Victoria's brand-new Egyptian rug.

"Shoot," I said meekly, bending over to pick up the plant.

Victoria looked mortified.

"Do you...do you have some paper towels?" I bleated. "I'll try to clean this up."

"We're not paying you to clean *that* up," she replied severely. "We're paying you to clean up this Jetpack mess."

I shook my head. "I just can't, OK? Frankly, I don't

want to. It's not worth the damage I'm doing to my marriage."

"Didn't your wife just get fired?"

"Yes, exactly! Because of me!" I thought about that for a second. "No wait, because of you! How could you do that to Maria?"

Victoria shrugged. "If you want to get ahead in PR, you've got to do what you've got to do."

"Sure, maybe in *dystopian* PR."

"I don't know what that means, and I don't care. Actually, the reason I brought up your wife's recent loss of a job is that I don't think you can afford to walk away from yours. Tell me, Blake, who's going to save for the future you want if you're both out of work?"

I hated to admit she had a point, but on the other hand, I wasn't sure if Maria and I would have a future together if I stayed in my job much longer. "I'm going home," I said resolutely. "I'll call in tomorrow to work out the details of my resignation."

Pursing her lips, Victoria held out her palm. "Then I guess I'll have to take your ID badge."

Admitting defeat hadn't felt great, but I figured that at least now I would be free. There would be victories to come.

I went to my office and swept the bobbleheads and other knickknacks on my desk into a reusable grocery bag. Carefully, I took down my autographed Funnyman Dan poster and carried the frame under my other arm. I leaned awkwardly to pick up my work bag and waddled out of the door like a fat penguin.

As I neared the exit, I started to feel pretty good. As if a weight had lifted from my shoulders. I was getting out. I was actually, finally, getting out of here!

I felt another rush of excitement when the crisp winter air touched my tongue. It reminded me of when I was a kid and I could just sense a snow day was coming to save me from another tense day at high school.

A low, robotic growl gave me an altogether different kind of chill. The mechanical beast with vicious violet eyes sat between me and the gate. Its wiry tail shot up in full alert.

What an idiot I'd been. Victoria had taken my badge, so the hound now considered me an intruder. I was as good as, well...Rico.

The beast rose from a haunch onto four legs and appeared ready to launch itself at me. Dropping the Funnyman Dan poster, I turned tail and sprinted back inside before it could get me.

Crack! The thing left a hairline fracture in the bullet-proof glass.

"You all right, man?" the guard at the door asked tepidly. He blew on a mug of steaming coffee, seemingly more concerned about the temperature of the drink than my near-death experience.

I pointed to the window, but the malicious beast was gone. I couldn't find the crack in the glass anymore, either, which must have been something to do with the light. "I'm fine. I was just going out for a quick breath of fresh air."

"You dropped something out there."

"That's OK," I said. No way was I going back out there. "If someone finds it, can you just keep it here at the desk?"

Confused, the guard pointed out the glass. "It's right there."

"Yeah, I know, but I'm kind of in a rush to get back to work."

Before he could argue further, I jogged off down the hallway back to Victoria's office.

She trilled happily at the news that I had changed my mind. "I guess you'd better get back to work."

"Right-o, boss!" I exclaimed with an emphatic thumbs-up.

One last crisis, I told myself as I left her office. Get through one last crisis, and then I could leave.

CHAPTER
TWENTY-FIVE

I HELD OFF putting my bobbleheads back on my desk.
Good PR reps always look for a way out—an
escape hatch from a particularly bad situation. Usually
one looks for the best way to get the client out of the situation. But me? I was thinking about myself.

The easiest way out, it seemed to me, was to let Jetpack
win. If I stopped trying to fight him, maybe the people
would boot Our Leader out of office. Then I wouldn't
even have to quit because there wouldn't be a job to leave!
Nobody would have to know I'd stopped trying.

Right?

The more I thought about it, the more I realized that I
couldn't go through with it. For one thing, I had my own
professional reputation to think about. If let my notorious client crash and burn, who would ever hire me to
represent them?

I wondered if it might be time to consider the "So
what?" defense. This can be a great option when all else
fails. Basically, it involves conceding to whatever attack
has been levied, but quickly following it with a "So
what?"

For example: "Yes, we deliberately excluded women
from this board of directors. Everyone does that. So
what?"

Or: "Yes, I allowed the patient to die. That happens sometimes in this line of work. So what?"

In this case, we could "confess" that Our Leader arrested his political rivals but say he's not exactly the first leader of a country to do such a thing. So what?

However, I wasn't sure I was ready to confess to something I genuinely wasn't sure the President had done. Believe it or not, the "So what?" defense requires a certain degree of honesty to be effective. Asking why it matters that you've done something you haven't really done can come across kind of douchey braggadocio. Like, "Hey dude, so what if I banged all those sorority bitches? Who hasn't?"

Plus, based on the way Our Leader had reacted to the claim before, it seemed like a pretty tall task to get him to even consider going along with such a plan.

I smacked my forehead and blurted, "Cripes!" It had just occurred to me that we should have used "So what?" to resolve the Project Milkman crisis. It would have been perfect! Our Leader had actually confessed to drugging people; all we would have had to do is ask why anyone needed to be upset about it. After all, the President had said he just wanted the best for his people, hadn't he? His intentions were golden. So what if a couple thousand people had gotten a little sleepy? So what if a few thousand others couldn't get enough of the milk?

Instead, I'd gone with the fake missile crisis. Sure, it had worked to get my boss out of trouble, but it had also launched me into a fight with Maria. I had backed myself into that same corner again.

Maybe I *was* losing it. I'd been feeling off my game ever since that damn hound pounced at me at Our

Leader's press conference. Things had only gotten worse when Al died. Without my confidence, I was acting on every dumb idea without thinking through the possible consequences. I'd lost my motivation and I was unwilling to do the hard work to correct my mistakes.

Enough whining, I told myself. Get back to work!

I guess I must have been tired because I fell asleep at my desk.

I say that to make it crystal clear what happened next was only a dream. It didn't happen—not really—but I'm talking about it to provide some context for what I did next. I never liked that thing in stories where something really messed up seems to happen, but then—in a gotcha twist—the protagonist just wakes up and is all like, "Oh thank God I didn't really kill Grandma with her own toothbrush!"

OK, so I remember closing my eyes to concentrate on the task at hand—finding a way out of this Jetpack mess.

"Give up, Blake," said a woman's voice. She said it like a siren asking a sailor to come ashore for a sex/murder party.

I looked at the door and saw Victoria. For some reason, she was wearing a jade dress tailored to fit tightly around her breasts, which looked much larger than in real life.

"I won't!" I yelled, jumping to my feet. "I'm not going to let you win!"

She sauntered closer and closer, until she was nearly pressed up against me and I could feel her warm breath on my face. Victoria's voice was deep and sultry as she hummed, "Give in."

In that instant, I wasn't married. I didn't even know Maria. I was in high school, or college, and horny as heck. I leaned in and kissed Victoria. It felt great.

I recalled the existence of Maria just as things were getting hot and heavy. I remembered that we had wanted to start a family. But now, because I was cheating on her with Victoria, it would never happen. I'd never spin my way out of something this treasonous. I'd ruined our lives in one unthinking moment.

The Communications Director mashed my naked forearm between two pincers of a toothy mandible. I screamed.

That's when I woke up. Per my disclaimer, it was all just a dream. I was alone in my office. I'd never kissed Victoria, but I still felt like I had done something wrong. Why was my subconscious cheating on my wife? If I could do that in a dream, did it mean that I wanted to in real life?

I decided to take it as a sign I needed to get my priorities straight. Maria was more important than this job. Way more important. Maybe I wasn't cheating on her with Victoria, but it didn't change the fact that I was spending far too much time away from my wife.

And so, with a deep breath, I got up and put on my coat.

The hallway lights were dim, and a robotic puck was slowly vacuuming the hallway. It occurred to me that Victoria had neglected to return my badge, so I stopped by her office to get it. She didn't answer when I knocked, and it looked dark through the frosted window. I tried opening the door, but it was locked.

No problem, I thought, *I'll just ask the guard for help getting out.* Anyway, part of me was glad not to have to see Victoria so soon after that dream.

I marched to the exit, where the guard was snoring. His arm hung loosely off the side of his swivel chair, with an empty mug dangling carelessly from one finger. My autographed Funnyman Dan poster was leaning up against the desk, but I decided that taking it would just slow me down. Scott could always bring it to me some day.

I felt weird about trying to wake up the guard, especially after the awkward exchange we'd had earlier, so I let him be and peered through the glass to check for the violet-eyed beast. Not seeing it, I tightened my shoelaces, took a deep breath, and opened the door.

A cold gust of air brought tears to my eyes. The gate looked about a mile away, but I still didn't see the hound.

I bolted for the exit. Halfway there, I started feeling relief. I was going to make it!

Then a terrible bark killed all hope. I willed myself not to look over my shoulder, but I could hear the thing's metal claws slapping against the sidewalk as it bounded toward my back. Its gnashing teeth made a sound like a closing bear trap.

My heart beat loudly through my chest.

Run, run, run!

Susan the gatekeeper gave me a sort of amused look as I barreled toward security. "Hey, Blake, you're here kind of late," she greeted, blissfully unaware of what was coming.

"Open the door!" I screamed. "Open the door!"

It swung open and I flew through. Susan must have finally noticed the hound, because she shut the gate fast. There was a loud crash as the steel beast collided with the steel fence.

I dropped to my knees and wheezed loudly. It felt as if someone had punched me in the stomach.

Susan laughed. "Big girl almost got you!"

When I tried to respond, phlegm fell out of my mouth.

"Oh, you know what must have happened?" said the guard like a regular Nancy Drew. "You're probably still carrying the red ID, right? Those have expired. There's a new one, now. It's blue."

CHAPTER
TWENTY-SIX

I FLAGGED A Wyde with my phone and was surprised to see the name "Robbie"—an actual human—come up in the app as my driver. When Woozle first got into the ride-share business a decade ago, founder Joe Steele was heralded for helping to boost the gig economy, creating tens of thousands of flexible jobs around the country. But only a few years in, Woozle made a splashy announcement about rolling out autonomous vehicles. Buried in the lede was the fact that actual drivers would no longer be required.

A tan compact car pulled up. The front passenger-side window lowered and a voice from inside the car called, "Blake?"

"That's..." I began to say as I opened the backseat door, but the driver's head swiveled unnaturally to face me, and I couldn't complete the sentence. Robbie was a robot. The face was waxy like a mannequin, with glass eyes and disturbingly red lips.

"Everything OK, Blake?" the dummy asked with some concern. I must have been giving it a weird look.

"Sorry. I'm, uh, I'm not used to someone actually sitting in the driver's seat."

"We rolled out last week to 10 percent of the fleet

as a pilot," Robbie explained. "Many customers said they didn't like feeling like they're riding in ghost cars."

"You're much better," I said sarcastically, figuring that robots didn't get sarcasm.

"Thanks!" it responded in delight.

I hoped Wyde would walk back this concept. It was pretty creepy. Still, after what I'd just been through, Robbie and the tan compact felt to me like Apollo commanding a golden chariot.

"Need to charge your phone?" the autonomous driver queried. "I've got all the cords."

"You certainly do, Robbie. You certainly do."

It was about midnight when we arrived at my brick row house. All the windows were black, which meant either that Maria had gone to bed angry at me—another thing we vowed never to do—or worse, that she'd packed up and left.

At least she had left on the porch light.

Robbie asked, "Is this your house?"

"It is," I said gravely.

The robot rotated its head to face me, and asked in the most pleasant way possible, "Are you going to get out?"

"I'm going to get out," I affirmed, pushing open the door. Then, thinking of my job, I declared, "This time I really am going to get out!"

"Please close the door gently on your way out."

"What? No, Robbie. Screw those people, I'm going to get out and slam the door right in their darn faces!"

"Please close the door gently on your way out."

"You know what? This has been a great ride. Five stars, Robbie!"

"You can use the app to rate—"

"Five stars!" I exclaimed again, slamming the door of the car.

I waited for the car to drive off. Then, with a deep breath, I marched up the walk to accept my punishment from Maria.

The heat switched on when I entered, and it felt as if it had been paused for some time. Turning on the lights, I called my wife's name. No response.

My phone beeped, but it was just asking me to rate my Wyde. I didn't feel like I had time for that, so I put the device back in my pocket and headed up the stairs to check if Maria was sleeping.

I performed my second-floor ritual of gazing into our makeshift storage room. It looked so devoid of life. There was a photo of us on the wall from around the time we'd decided to have a kid. I made up a caption that I wasn't sure was funny or sad: *Here's some proof that Mommy and Daddy were not always so old, frail, and helpless. Sorry you have to take care of us now!*

I resumed my climb up to our third-floor master bedroom. I didn't see the familiar lump beneath the covers.

When I went back downstairs, I saw a note on the little stand in the foyer where we kept unread mail.

> *You probably won't see this note before I get home, but I went out to chase a lead at Woozle. There's some leftover ravioli in the fridge.*

Woozle? What was she doing at Woozle? Revenge? I knew she had blamed her firing on the new ownership, but it didn't seem like Maria to go after a story based on feelings—she was better than that.

Thinking back to our phone conversation, I recalled a moment when her voice took on the questioning tone of an investigative journalist. I'd been too focused on the immediate problem of Our Leader's speech to give it much notice, but what was it she had said? That Jetpack's voice and mannerisms were familiar?

I fired up Triple N-Demand on the TV and watched Maria's full, unedited interview with the idiot knight. I must have played that grating interview ten times before I understood why she'd gone to Woozle. I wasn't 100 percent on the voice, but there was something in the face that gnawed at me. There was a point in the interview when Maria had made a lame joke about Jetpack literally appearing out of the blue. For one fleeting second, his lips curled upward to form a buck-toothed smile. It was a smile I *recognized*.

Not totally believing it, I checked one last thing. I did a search online for *"Dark as Day" AND "Joe Steele."* Although I'd never played it, the Woozle CEO's obsession with the first-person shooter was legendary. The first of several articles that came up included a big picture of his avatar. It wasn't a silver knight, but the tuxedoed super spy *was* wearing a jetpack.

Suddenly, I was feeling as giddy as a little kid who knows exactly what he's getting for his Annual Late-December Holiday Celebration.

CHAPTER
TWENTY-SEVEN

M ARIA DIDN'T PICK up when I called, so I texted to say I was coming to meet her, then called another Wyde. I prayed my wife wouldn't do anything stupid without me. It would be so much better to do something stupid together.

This car didn't even have a robot driver, so it was a pretty uneventful ride to Dupont Circle. I remembered eating lunch there with my parents one time when I was a kid and we visited the capital. Back then, it was a little park with a fountain in the middle, but now a girthy silo stretched erect from the round plot of land into the night sky. Emblazoned in big white letters at the top of the skyscraper was one made-up word: *Woozle*. The tech company's lawyers had somehow found a loophole in zoning restrictions that limited other buildings to only five stories.

Woozle had moved its headquarters here about five years ago, right around the time Congress was becoming anxious about how large the company was getting. Joe Steele had decided it was time to establish a presence much closer to the decision makers. He packed his grand new home with lobbyists who periodically streamed outside to buy steak frites for Senate aides. The strategy had helped Steele avoid privacy regulations and, more recently, to win approval for the company's massive acquisition of Triple N.

"Blake!" came a sharp whisper.

I swiveled to my right and saw our white hover sedan parked on the side of the road. We'd installed privacy glass to avoid Maria being recognized by her fans, but I would have recognized that hunk of junk anywhere.

I jogged around to the street side and opened the passenger door. Maria, a long-lens camera hanging from her neck, didn't look pleased to see me. "What are you doing here?"

"I got your note, and I wanted to help."

She raised an eyebrow. "What about your job?"

"I'm not going back there."

My wife laughed. It was devastating.

"No, really! That so-called 'Hero Pup' nearly killed me, but I made it through the gate, and I raced home to see you. You weren't there, but I saw your note." I took a moment to inhale. "Didn't you get my text?"

Maria shook her head. "I didn't bring my phone. Wait, you mean Violet?"

"What?"

"The Hero Pup. Remember the naming contest?"

"They named her *Violent*?"

"Not Violent... Violet! Like the color. And no, it doesn't contain a silent *n*."

"Ha, ha."

"They even made a web series with a catchy theme song," she continued excitedly. "It goes, 'Violet, the Hero Pup! Don't cross her, or she'll *ruff* you up!'"

"Clever," I deadpanned.

My failure to be impressed didn't wipe the big smile

off Maria's face. "You probably couldn't tell because I was singing it aloud, but 'ruff you up' was a pun."

"I got it."

"Because dogs go, 'Ruff!'"

"I got it!"

"How do you not know about this? It's government propaganda gone viral! Everybody knows the tune and everybody loves it."

I shrugged. "Web videos and social media are more Debbie's territory."

Maria looked confused. "Who's Debbie?"

"She's our Social Media Director."

"I've never heard you mention her before."

"Well, she's not...I mean, usually, she's not that ..."

"That woman deserves a *promotion*, Blake. I'm serious."

I asked why Maria hadn't brought her phone.

"Well, I don't want Woozle tracking my location when I'm literally staking out their headquarters, do I?"

"Oh."

Her expression turned to one of disappointment. "You brought yours, didn't you?"

Guiltily, I brought the phone out of my pocket. "Well, I needed it for the Wyde."

"You took a Wyde here?! Blake, tell me you know who owns Wyde."

"Oh crap." I noticed a hover bus coming down the street, so—thinking fast—I opened the window and tossed the device out in front of the mammoth vehicle. The thing got sucked up into the heavy magnets that kept the bus afloat.

"Blake!" admonished Maria. "You could have just turned it off."

Painfully, it hit me that I'd just lost a barely three-month-old device that had cost nearly a thousand dollars. Stupid.

We sat for a long time in silence, but I was just counting my blessings that Maria was even tolerating my presence in the car.

"That was pretty smart of you to connect Jetpack with Joe Steele," I offered.

She flashed a conspiratorial smile. "So you see it, too."

The implications were more immense than the man's dick-shaped headquarters. Jetpack had claimed that Our Leader was somehow responsible for the disappearance of Steele, but if Steele was the stupid knight, it meant he was lying. If he was lying about that, he very well could have been lying about the other disappearances. Although, that of course begged the question of what did happen to the likes of Jason Stonybrook, Funnyman Dan, and the others.

I shook my head. "I don't get his motivation, though. Woozle's doing great."

"That's what I came here to find out," said Maria. "But the moron at the front desk told me Joe was missing and asked if I'd seen the news. Can you believe he asked *me* if I'd seen the news?"

I reacted big. "Unbelievable!"

"I told him I was going to wait in the lobby anyway, but the idiot said that would be loitering and I had to leave. Anyway, I thought I'd wait here in the car and watch the door."

I scratched my head. "You really think Steele is going

to just come walking out when he's got everyone thinking he's in a dungeon somewhere beneath the Compound?"

"Obviously not, but I thought maybe someone else important would come out, and I can at least get them to talk."

I shook my head. "There's no time for that. Jetpack's protest march is hours away, and if it happens...well, I think Our Leader might do something pretty horrible."

Maria's face became grim. Then she turned away, toward the window. "It's Victoria, isn't it?"

The question was like a punch to the gut. How could she know what I had dreamed?

But then I saw the Communications Director, too. "What's *she* doing here?"

Maria snapped a couple photos as Victoria went straight through Woozle HQ's big glass doors to security. The man at the front desk unlocked the elevator for her without even checking her ID. He'd recognized her! She'd been here before!

"Why would...?" Maria wondered aloud.

"I don't know," I said, "but we're going to find out."

Something buzzed by my ear as we approached the grand entrance to Woozle HQ. I swatted and missed.

"Hey, watch it!"

Maria turned to me. "Did that bee just tell you to watch it?"

It took me a few seconds to realize it wasn't an insect at all. "It's one of our drones! Scott, Is that you?"

"In the living thorax!" replied the tinny voice. "Mel's here, too."

Maria scrunched her eyes the way she did on TV with particularly vexing interviewees. "Who?"

"The overseer who works below us," I tried to explain. "I'm not talking about her rank—she's pretty high up, actually. But she works many levels below us—physically—in the sub-basement."

Maria stared blankly at me. I pulled her close and whispered into her ear, "I think she and Scott have a thing."

That tidbit earned a raise of my wife's eyebrows. Grinning ear to ear, she cooed, "Awww..."

"What?" asked Scott. "What did you tell her?"

"Nothing, nothing," I said dismissively. "So, what are you doing here? How did you find me?"

"We've been watching you since you got away from Violet."

It bugged me a little—no pun intended—that I was the last one to know about the result of the naming contest that was my idea to begin with.

"Speaking of fun names," I said to Maria. "What should we call a drone that is both Mel Copps and Scott Jones?"

My wife grinned. "Skell? Mott?"

"Skeleton Moans?" I offered.

"Kind of long, and you made up a couple syllables."

"You snickered, though."

She winked. "Let's stay focused on the matter at hand. Do you guys know why Victoria is here?"

"I was going to ask you guys," Scott replied.

I'd thought there was a chance Victoria could be here

on government business, but this seemed to confirm she was freelancing.

Mel harrumphed. "I've just asked a team to pull up surveillance records on her from the last year. I'll let you know if we find anything concerning."

"So, we're not going to wait outside the door all night, right?" asked Scott. "Take us with you inside."

I frowned. "Hey, man, I don't know if we should work together on this one. I mean, I quit. I'm not working for Our Leader anymore. It's not why I'm here."

"I know, and I'm sorry I tried to stop you, man. The fact you're finally getting out just shows again which one of us is the smart one. But we can still help each other. Mel and I can record everything those bastards say to you. Maria can use the footage for TV, and I can use it to get my job back."

With a rush of panic, Maria looked down her chest. "Shoot! I left my camera in the car." Shaking her head, she looked at me and said, "Footage *would* be nice."

"Anyway," declared Scott, "even if we're not working together, we can still be friends, right?"

I nodded. "Yeah, we can still be friends."

"Gross," commented Maria.

"Don't listen to her, Scott," I said with an annoyed, sideways glance. "Now, get inside me and let's do it."

I couldn't help but yip as the drone penetrated my ear.

"Oh, don't be such a little bitch," Scott snapped.

I asked Maria for her purse, then told her to wait outside until I signaled. With the bug in place, I jogged through the doors and straight to security with my wife's bag.

"May I help you, sir?" asked the nimrod at the desk.

He had on a TV infomercial about cutlery to which he looked eager to return.

I pretended to be out of breath. OK, so maybe I really was out of breath. "Have you seen my boss, Victoria Chu? She was coming here but left her purse behind. I'm her assistant, Blake Hamner." I flashed my old government badge, the red one. "If you could just let me up, I'll bring it to her and then be on my way."

The guard studied the purse, then the badge, then me for good measure. I could feel my heart beating.

"This is your plan?" said Mel.

Scott defended me. "A good story can get you anywhere. That's what Blake always says."

"Your badge is expired," said the guard, reaching for his desk phone. "I'm going to have to call up and ask."

"Oh for crying out loud," snapped Overseer Copps.

I shivered as the bug zoomed out of my ear canal. The guard was too focused on dialing to see the miniature robot coming. A quick zap made the thug's eyes slide back and he fell forward into his desk. The bee popped its head into a USB port on the guard's computer. A few seconds later, the elevator doors opened.

The bug twittered excitedly, but I couldn't make out any words until it re-entered my ear.

"How about later?" Mel offered suggestively.

Resisting the urge to vomit, I signaled to Maria to come inside and we rushed toward the elevator. But when we got inside, I was baffled to find no grid of numbered buttons. Not that I knew which one I needed to press, but still.

The doors closed and we began to ascend.

"Uh, where is the elevator taking us exactly?" I asked.

"When I hacked the guard's computer, I saw that Victoria went to the fortieth floor," said Copps. "So, I set the elevator to take us there directly."

CHAPTER
TWENTY-EIGHT

THE BEST PR plans have three steps—no more, no less—and I thought I had a doozy. Step One: Get out of the elevator! Step Two: Tiptoe down a bland corridor and find the door to Joe Steele's office. Step Three: Send Drone Skeleton Moans through the keyhole to capture a (hopefully) damning conversation with Victoria.

The plan failed pretty much immediately. When the elevator opened, there was nothing but night sky on the other side. Holding the OPEN DOORS button while grasping tightly to the jamb for support, I peered in wonder at the sparkling streetlights many stories below.

"Something's not right," said Maria.

I laughed at the understatement. "You think?"

"No, I mean, it's the middle of winter, and I don't feel even a little bit cold."

"We'll take a look," offered the mechanical bee, now featuring a tinnier version of Mel's voice. It buzzed out of my ear canal, flew up into the sky, and collided with an invisible barrier. "What the—?" Diving toward the street, the drone crashed into another obstacle where the floor should have been. "Hey!" Buzzing erratically back in my direction, the bug cried, "I don't think this is real!"

I didn't have a chance to respond because, at that

moment, Victoria Chu entered the scene from around the corner of what looked like an adjacent office building. She was clutching a goblet of champagne and looking pleased with herself as she strode through the air. "Blake Hamner and Maria Worthington—to what do we owe the displeasure?"

"You can *fly*?" squealed the bug with Scott inside.

"She can't fly," Maria replied patiently. "This is an illusion."

Something clicked and, like a TV shutting off, the color drained from the room. The next thing I knew, we were standing in a ballroom so blindingly white, it felt like floating in a void. Jetpack himself emerged from behind the far-corner wall that used to be an office building, holding another glass of bubbly. The weird knight took a yellow pistol from his belt and pointed it at us. The plastic weapon looked straight out of a bad sci-fi film.

"What is that supposed to be? A ray gun?" I chided.

He smiled slightly just before firing. To my surprise, I felt actual heat as a brilliant bolt of yellow burst by my head. There was a short sizzle, like a mosquito caught in an electric trap.

"Oh my God," I yelped. "Is my hair OK?"

Maria scoffed. "Since when do you care about how you look?"

Jetpack pulled the barrel to his lips and pretended to blow away the smoke.

It seemed like a great opening for Scott to make a sex joke, so I found his lack of reaction suspicious. I located the bug's carcass sizzling on the ground. Victoria stepped forward to crush the charred remnants with the steel-tipped heel of her stiletto.

"You killed Skeleton Moans!" I cried. My heart was beating wildly. True, Scott and Mel weren't physically inside, but somehow this still felt like losing my friends. Well, one friend. I guess Mel was never really my friend. Either way, it was bad, because the whole point of bringing the drone along was to get damning footage.

"What is this place?" asked Maria. At least one of us had maintained some level of cool.

"Let me show you," said Jetpack. "HR, become a rain forest."

The room became a rain forest. Dew sparkled on the fiery petal of the largest flower I'd ever seen, while a symphony of wild birds bobbed and weaved among the tropical green giants. Maria leaned over a big leaf to consider a neon-yellow tree frog.

"Welcome to HR," said Jetpack.

"Human Resources?" I asked with horror.

"Holographic Reality," sneered the knight.

"An illusion," declared Maria again. "Not unlike the mask hiding your true identity—Joe Steele!"

With a chuckle, Jetpack brought his hands up to lift the futuristic knight's mask off his fuzzy blond head. Frowning, he patted the sides of his suit. "Shit, where are my glasses?"

Victoria brought him a pair of thick-framed specs. Joe wiped the lenses with a microfiber cloth and placed them carefully atop the bridge of his nose.

"So, what if you know?" Steele whined in the nerd knight's true, squeaky voice. "I never intended to keep my identity secret forever. You see, when Woozle does well, the world does well. A more...sympathetic...president can take Woozle—and therefore the world—to the next level!"

Trying to keep a straight face, I said, "Whoa, wait, what? World? Why Woozle?"

"Why Woozle?" he returned. "Well, why not Woozle? Woozle is the future! Woozle—"

"He's mocking you, Joe," said Victoria, ruining my fun. "Blake just likes to alliterate."

Things were starting to click. Scott and I had been right to blame Victoria for just about everything that had gone wrong lately. First, she'd taken advantage of the hound crisis to make herself look good and take Scott's job. I could see now how she might have created that opportunity.

I pointed my finger accusingly at the former intern. "The day before the Hound got loose, you helped Debbie with a photo shoot with the Hound Handlers..."

Victoria clasped her hands together like a praying mantis. "I might have placed a little bug in its ear."

Steele smirked. "That bug gave me direct access to the machine's brain. I showed it a way out of the Compound, but that's all! I didn't tell it where to go after that."

"That thing murdered two people, you dweeb!" I erupted. "Your hands are certainly not clean. And I'm guessing that was you up in the roofs filming our tour of the Project Milkman project?"

"No, it was *Spider-Man*," jeered the young tech executive. "Of course it was me."

Victoria had sent Scott and me to those rural towns just to set us up for Jetpack's big movie. "What about the New Year's Eve party?" I asked her. "I know about the poison in Our Leader's champagne. I presume you poured in the vial?"

"Great Scott!" she responded with a sarcastic gasp. "Yes. I slipped him the bottle while he was getting ready for the party. He got through about half of it before he started feeling ill."

That's what Victoria and Steele had been guffawing about at the party.

The unmasked Jetpack grinned. "My live video of that embarrassing performance would have gone viral even if I hadn't pumped up its visibility on Woozler."

"Which you did again later for every positive wooze about Jetpack!" I charged. "Debbie had mentioned something looked funny. Speaking of which, where's Funnyman Dan?"

"And the *other* prisoners," said Maria, giving me the side-eye for momentarily forgetting them.

It stood to reason that Steele's people had been abducting Our Leader's favorite foils to create speculation that the President was putting his enemies in a secret government prison...or worse. Then, Jetpack introduced himself to the people to confirm what everyone was already starting to worry about Our Leader.

"Oh, you don't need to worry about *them*," said Joe, dead-eyed. "They're all in heaven."

Maria glared. "You murdered them?!"

"What?" He seemed genuinely taken aback. "Oh, I see how you could—no, I meant that they're *simply* in heaven right now in Woozle's other HR spaces. I gave them all exactly what they wanted. Jason Stonybrook is sitting at a virtual executive desk, surrounded by scantily clad yes-women—"

"Wait," I said, "didn't he run on family values?"

"He's married!" protested Maria.

Steele shrugged. "Funnyman Dan has a virtual audience that laughs at every one of his dumb jokes," he continued. "Antonia Daniels is pretending to be a super-soldier in a war simulation, for some reason. For what it's worth, I can assure you they're all well-fed. I didn't want to torture anyone. I just needed them out of the way for a few weeks."

"You might claim to be treating your prisoners well, but a lot of people *will* get hurt," I said. "Our Leader is planning to send in troops to break up your rally."

The unmasked knight shrugged. "I never said *nobody* would get hurt. Anyway, it will end there. When the soldiers attack the crowd, that will be the final straw for the nation. Our revolution will be assured!"

Maria threw up her hands in consternation. "I still don't understand. Why are you doing any of this? Your company's been doing well, maybe even better since Our Leader became president. I couldn't find any history of you and Prawnmeijer not getting along."

"I'm doing this because I am a patriot," said Steele. He took a swig of champagne, presumably to let that claim sink in, but the nerd's loud slurping undermined the statement's gravity. "I saw my country descending into a dystopian nightmare. At first, I thought, what can anyone do to stop this? Then, I realized I'm not just anyone—I am the head of the world's greatest tech company!"

"What you are is a psychopath!" I exclaimed.

Jetpack shrugged. "It might seem that way to the unenlightened."

I nearly charged, but Maria held me back. "What will you do when the people find out what you've done?" she asked him.

Steele laughed. "Who's going to tell them? You don't work for Triple N, and even if you gabbed to someone there, it would never get on the air. I own Triple N. I control the message now!"

"Our Leader might be interested to know what you're doing," I volunteered, "not to mention that his Communications Director has been working with the enemy."

Victoria made a face. "Whatever, Ham-ner."

"The *n* is silent!" Maria and I shouted at the same time.

"Actually, that's why we're celebrating," said Steele. "Victoria won't be returning to the Compound. We're already onto the next phase of the plan."

They clinked glasses.

"So, wait," I asked Victoria. "Are you actually into him? Or are you just a career climber?"

"At least I'm not stuck in a dead-end job," she spit back.

"Ouch," I said, frowning. "But not anymore. I'm quitting."

She snickered. "Sure you are."

Joe's head swung toward Ms. Chu. "But, wait, you are into me, right?"

"Right," she assured him a little too quickly.

"So then, what are you going to do with us?" asked Maria. It was the question I'd been avoiding.

Steele laughed haughtily. "Actually, I was thinking about sending you on that honeymoon the two of you have never managed to take."

"What? How did you—?"

"Oh, come now," teased Steele. "Woozle tracks everywhere you go on the Internet. Both of you check travel websites for deals on tropical getaways at least once a week, and yet neither of you have ever pulled the trigger. So, how about this? I'll fly you anywhere you want to go, all expenses paid, for three months. Just long enough to complete our takeover. In exchange for your silence, you can even have cushy jobs with Woozle when you come back. To be honest, I could use more people with your communications talents."

"We'd never work for you," I declared.

"Maria already worked for me, at Triple N," he corrected. "And Blakey, I know you don't like your job. Bitch, bitch, bitch—it's all your phone's 'Woozle assistant' ever hears! So, why don't you let me win? You won't have to quit Our Leader, and you'll have a job already lined up. Talk about job security!"

I had thought about that before. I looked into Maria's eyes and saw she wanted the same thing as I did. "OK, fine."

"Great!" Steele snapped his fingers and the room morphed into a tropical beach. "You can start your holiday right away. I think there's mojito mix in the back."

Maria and I stared dumbfounded into the gently lapping ocean waves. Our hosts jogged around us to enter a weird beach shack with automatic sliding doors. On closer inspection, I realized it was the elevator.

"Don't worry," said Steele as the doors closed. "If you're good, I'll send you to the real thing after the protest. Think of this as a demo of a wonderful future with Woozle."

CHAPTER
TWENTY-NINE

I RETURNED FROM a holographic tiki bar with two physical cups of coffee. Handing one to Maria, I sat with her on sand that felt like hard tile, and we looked into a sea that couldn't spray any water.

"It's kind of nice," said Maria.

I shrugged. "It *looks* nice."

She cracked a smile. "So, how would you pitch this?"

I grinned. "Tired of leaving your sofa even to have a good time? Now you can get away without going away!"

My wife giggled. "In just twenty-four monthly payments of one thousand, nine hundred, and ninety-nine dollars and ninety-nine cents!"

"We'll even throw in this spatula for free!"

Maria snorted. "A spatula?"

I shrugged. "It's a funny word. *Spatula*!"

"You're weird, Ham." She put her arm around my back.

Maria and I had never seriously considered Steele's offer, of course. We had just wanted Joe and Victoria to leave so that we could try to find a way out. It wasn't going well. We had attempted to open the elevator, but it wouldn't budge. We'd checked every wall of the ballroom for cracks but found the place more secure than a padded cell. There weren't even any windows.

At least the coffee kept us awake. The sun—the real one—would be coming up soon. Jetpack's protest would be starting in hours. Our Leader would send in his army. Bloodshed would ensue.

I touched my wife's hand. "I'm sorry, by the way."

Maria looked at me. She wasn't saying anything, just waiting for me to say more.

"I know I've let work dominate my life. I thought if I could get through one more crisis, I'd spend more time on us."

"There's always one more crisis, Blake."

"I know. I put our relationship on cruise control. I've made us put off starting a family."

"And you're fat."

I smiled slightly. "And I'm fat."

Maria gripped my hand. "Have you really been looking at travel websites once a week?" she asked.

"At least. You do that, too?"

"I've been wanting to look with you, but I thought you'd think I was nagging you about the honeymoon."

"No, it's definitely overdue."

She kissed me. "Do you...do you still want to have a baby with me?"

"Yes. I think I've just... This world is so screwed up, and all I've done with my life is mess it up even worse. I think part of me has feared bringing new life into a place like this. I don't want my kid to see me in this job where all I'm doing is creating more problems. I don't want them to see me as just another cog in a broken system."

Maria's eyes looked dewy, but she was smiling. "You don't have to be a cog, Blake."

I pondered the ocean.

She took my hand. "It's not just you who has been working too hard. Maybe it's for the best that I got fired. Ever since Steele bought Triple N, the place has really gone down the tube. Maybe this is a chance for both of us to reassess what's important in our lives."

I kissed her. "I've missed you, Maria."

She kissed me. "You really are a ham, Ham."

"There's something I need to tell you, though. I kind of cheated on you."

She withdrew. "What? Kind of?"

"Well, it was only a dream, but still."

She actually laughed at me—I couldn't believe it! "With whom did you cheat on me in this dream?"

"Victoria, but..."

Maria snorted merrily. "Veronica?!"

I couldn't stop my arms from flailing as I talked. "I know! I don't even like her! But in the dream, it was like I'd forgotten all about you, or maybe that we'd broken up. I only remembered you when it was too late. And then I was just so upset with myself."

My wife grinned at my pain.

"You're not mad?"

She shook her head. "Dreams are weird! I cheat on you all the time in dreams—mostly with boys from high school. Anyway, it's cute you were upset."

I kissed her, then stopped. "Boys, plural?"

Maria pushed me onto my back and put her leg over my body. "Don't worry about it."

Bang! Our serene ocean view exploded.

When the smoke cleared, it looked as though the night had cut a hole in the day. Gliding a frigid breeze, a mechanical bee rushed toward Maria and me. "'Sup?" it said.

"Scott! Mel!" exclaimed Maria, rising to her feet. "I thought y'all got fried."

"A million more drones where that one came from," replied Mel. "Sorry it took a while to get back here, though. Had to call in a favor to blast the wall."

"This whole thing was for nothing!" I shouted. My ears were ringing and I could barely hear my own voice. "We don't have any evidence that Steele's up to no good!"

"Or do we?" asked Maria with a little mischief in her voice.

I stared at my wife blankly. I had thought Jetpack had destroyed the bee before it could take any truly incriminating footage.

She dipped a manicured hand into her purse and brought out a basic voice recorder.

"You got it?"

"The whole thing."

I kissed her. "I love you so much."

She winked. "I love you, too."

"You guys are real cute," said Mel inside the bug. "Maybe you could take *me* out sometime?"

"Uh," said Maria.

I waved my hands and explained, "She's talking to Scott. I think. Right?"

"Oh, she's not just *talking* to me," said Scott, and I

almost threw up. "Hey, maybe we should—ooh, right there, yeah—plan a double date sometime?"

"Um," said Maria, "maybe let's focus?"

Crossing my arms in a vain attempt to keep warm, I wandered over to the big hole in the wall. The dawn of a new day normally brings cheer, but seeing the sun rise filled me with dread. "We don't have much time. Scott. Is Our Leader awake yet?"

"I'm not sure he ever went to sleep. He's been freaking out about this protest. Keeps asking the Handlers to make sure the hounds are ready to go."

"He's probably just hungry," I said. "Get him a bowl of cereal."

The Scott-drone bobbed silently for a few seconds. "Wait, are you serious?"

"Make it with *milk*," I said.

"How else would I make it?"

I gave the bug a hard stare.

"Oh! The milk! I'll get right on it."

"And get some police here right away to search the building. Steele said he'd stuck all the missing folks in holographic dungeons like this. Maybe they're in the building."

"On it," said Mel. "So, how about we get you guys back to the Compound?"

"Sure," said Maria, taking a few steps toward the giant hole in the wall. "But, uh, how are we supposed to get down?"

"Oh, that's easy," said the Chief Overseer.

A black hovercraft descended into view. Standing in the open doorway, the pilot beckoned us with a magnanimous wave of his meatball sub.

CHAPTER
THIRTY

T HE FIRST LIGHT of morning revealed a mob streaming into the Mall and gathering around a black stage in the place where Jetpack had made his sensational first appearance. Many wore silver-painted cardboard jetpacks over puffer jackets. Some carried large, handwritten signs with messages like JETPACK REVOLUTION! and NOT OUR LEADER.

A long red-carpeted aisle meant for TV crews extended toward a massive stage. It featured a porcelain backdrop emblazoned with the retro-futuristic logo I'd previously seen as sticker graffiti around the city. The combination reminded me of the urinal where I'd pissed all over one.

Someone then shouted, "He's here!"

The sheep squinted heavenward to see their would-be savior. At first, you could barely see him against the brightness of the rising sun. However, as Jetpack descended below the fiery orb, he became a kind of sparkling star in his own right.

What a loser.

I wasn't there in person, thank goodness. All the chemical hand warmers in the world couldn't convince me to stand outside at dawn in the middle of winter. You'd think that in a time of hover cars, scientists would have figured out a better way to keep people toasty in the colder months, but I guess that's just the world we live in. In any case, we—that is, Maria, Scott, Mel, Debbie, and I—watched the event unfold from the warmth of Our Leader's Compound.

Mel went to the window to close the blinds. I guess the sun was making the screen a little tough to see, but I think it might have had more to do with the Chief Overseer's discomfort with natural light. She was wearing a pair of sunglasses, too.

Victoria—yes, Victoria—was hosting the event for Triple N. The network switched to a shot of her walking backward along the red carpet toward the stage. "It's the moment we've all been waiting for," she commentated melodramatically. "Jetpack has *arrived*."

"Yeah, he has," said Scott, sticking out his tongue.

"Ew," replied Maria.

The camera followed Victoria through the throng of protesters. They looked too enraptured with the man floating down onto the stage to realize they were on live TV. Usually the channel got a few waves or shout-outs to Mom, but not here.

"Just look at everyone," enthused the fake TV reporter. "The excitement is palpable."

"I'll show you palpable," sneered Scott.

Maria gave him a look. "Excuse me?"

"What? We don't like her, right?"

"Ignore him," I instructed Maria. "Scott probably doesn't know what he means by that, either."

He shrugged.

Our Leader was having a deliriously good sleep from all the milk he'd had to drink. Scott had given him the cereal like I had instructed. What I hadn't counted on was Our Leader enjoying it so much. Apparently, he'd asked for seconds, then thirds, declaring he'd never had cereal so good before. So yeah, he'd been out for a while, and I wasn't exactly looking forward to when he finally woke up.

I dipped a spoon into my own breakfast, a suspiciously cold oatmeal my wife had termed overnight oats. What I'd wanted was a jelly donut, or really any kind of pastry. I wondered if Sarah's Diner was open yet.

"Oh god, here it comes," croaked Maria, pointing at the screen.

Victoria was now facing the stage. But behind her, creeping up the red carpet through the crowd, was a low, dark thing. The cameraman seemed to see it first because he began to step away from the host, refocusing the lens into the distance to get a better view.

Irritably, Victoria complained, "Hey, I'm over here. What do you think you're—?"

She turned back to look...and shrieked. A beast! And not just any beast.

"Violet the Hero Pup!" a little boy sang giddily to his dad. "Don't cross her, or she'll *ruff* you up!"

Some other protesters turned to look, then began tapping shoulders of the people next to them. That's when our purple-eyed machine charged. Blissfully unaware of the hound's violent true nature, the people looked strangely pleased to see it.

Victoria, however, knew exactly what was up, and let out a blood-curdling scream.

"This better work," I said uneasily. I'm no murderer.

Sensing my thoughts, Maria put her arm around me. "Don't worry," she said, but she was shaking.

The cameraman continued to shoot—and scream—as the hound charged toward them. Victoria looked like a statue, as frozen as I had been when it had attacked at the Rose Garden press conference.

Some folks chanted, "Hero Pup! Hero Pup! Hero Pup!"

Violet pounced! But as the creature neared the apex of its arc, an armored figure dropped onto the carpet between dog and woman.

There was a collective gasp from the crowd. Jetpack! Right on schedule.

The stupid knight caught the beast in midair. Our hound tried to bite through Jetpack's armor, but the suit was too strong. Joe Steele was never one to create things just for looks, so naturally he had engineered the crap out of his Jetpack outfit. Not only did it provide great defense, but it also enhanced his strength. He tapped into that power now to crush the dog's head as if it was an empty can of soda. As her bright eyes blinked out for the last time, the dying hound emitted the most pathetic dog's yelp that Debbie could find on the Internet.

The crowd groaned as Jetpack dropped the beast onto the crimson walkway. He dusted his hands to stunned silence.

"Fear not—" he started to say, but someone booed.

He looked confused as more and more people joined in. Soon it was a chorus of that one low note. "Booooooooooo!"

Jetpack/Steele protested, "B-but I saved Veronica's life!"

My former boss scowled. "Victoria."

Something splattered off the knight's jetpack.

Scott laughed. "Was that an egg? Why did anyone even think to bring that?"

A tomato glanced off Victoria's shoulder, staining her white blouse.

Jetpack pulled her close and lit up his tin knapsack.

"He's trying to escape!" yelled Maria.

"Don't worry," said Mel, tapping the side of her shades. "I've got them."

A dark cloud buzzed into frame and chased the pair up into the sky. The camera could only zoom in so much, but we could clearly see the moment when the swarm of bee drones reached them and the dumb knight's jetpack short-circuited. They swerved jerkily about the sky like a balloon someone forgot to tie, then Jetpack crashed helmet-first into the giant porcelain backdrop. The armor protected him and Victoria from the full impact, but they both looked pretty dizzy after sliding down the glorified urinal and onto the stage floor.

To loud cheers, Our Leader's soldiers rushed onto the stage and apprehended the pair of traitors.

Maria nudged me. "Blake, you're holding your breath."

I let the air out in one gust and breathed in the sweet smell of victory—or more likely, the sweet smell of donuts coming into the Comms Situation Room in the arms of a new intern who I'd never seen before in my life but who I now believed was the best intern we'd ever had.

"The Hammer strikes back!" exclaimed Scott, pumping his arms. "Looks like you won that bet with Victoria."

"We're not finished yet," I teased. "Ladies and gentlemen, let's go live!"

I reached for a jelly donut, but Maria slapped my hand away.

CHAPTER
THIRTY-ONE

W E WENT LIVE in the Green Room, which is exactly what it sounds like. It's a broadcasting studio with lawn-colored walls, upon which we can digitally paint whatever the situation demands. Scott often used it for Our Leader's non-denominational holiday messages. The most recent saw Prawnmeijer singing "Jingle Bells" while riding a digital horse-drawn sleigh through an animated winter wonderland. The fan base loved that kind of thing.

For this morning's broadcast, we used a background that mimicked a TV news set. It had a way of lending more authenticity to whatever nonsense the person standing in front of it was saying. It was exciting to be able to use it for real news, for once.

Maria took a seat behind the news desk. I was about to motion to the cameraman to start shooting, when she said to wait.

"What?" I asked.

"Did you tell Triple N this time?"

She was referring, of course, to the recent debacle in which no one had aired Our Leader's speech live.

"What's the point? Joe Steele probably told them not to show anything from us after what just happened."

With a long sigh, my wife got out her phone. "Hi,

Sally? Maria. I know! Crazy, right? Mm-hmm. Mm-hmm. So, I'm calling because I'm about to go live from the Compound. Can you make sure they show it on Triple N? Thanks, Sally."

"That's all it took?" I asked, a little bewildered and more than a little impressed. "They're going to show it?"

Maria smiled as if it was no big deal. "Sally's going to pull some strings."

"And how long's that going to—"

My wife's phone beeped twice. "They're ready," she said. "And so am I."

With a shrug, I turned to the cameraman and told him to start shooting.

I had offered to write Maria a script, but she said she didn't need one. I shouldn't have been worried. It took my news anchor wife less than five minutes to lay out how Joe Steele had smeared Our Leader, including by framing him for the multiple high-profile disappearances, and then put on the Jetpack identity as a ruse to steal power so that he could make more money for his giant corporation.

"I've got a recording to prove it," said the reporter. "Run the tape."

I ran the tape.

Debbie tapped me vigorously on the shoulder while it played. Social, it appeared, was going nuts. "Hashtag #fire," she whispered.

I offered a thumbs-up.

"The police found Steele's prisoners locked individually in Holographic Reality rooms at Woozle HQ," said Maria, wrapping up the report. "They were found in mostly good health, though the experience with HR left some complaining of thumping headaches that lasted for hours."

Scott came into the room just as the cameras went off. Despite our victory, his face carried a distinct look of worry. Approaching Debbie and me, he said, "Our Leader just woke up...and he wants to see all of us."

I took a deep breath and followed Scott and Debbie into the Throne Room. Our Leader sat childlike, with his feet up on the seat and arms wrapped around his knees. When he saw me, he gushed, "Ham-ham!"

I'm pretty sure he'd never called me that before.

Our Leader jumped out of the throne and ran to me with arms extended. "Hugs!" he exclaimed, hugging me.

It was a long hug.

"Deb-deb!" bleated the President, turning to the Social Media Director for the next embrace.

"Smiling cat with heart-eyes emoji!" she returned.

"Scotty!"

"I'm kind of sweaty—" said my friend, but Our Leader hugged him anyway.

"You all saved me! Oh, how can I ever thank you?"

This was unexpected. Our Leader was being...nice?

"Hey, you didn't happen to bring me any more of that delicious cereal, did you? That cereal was amazing. I feel great! I fell asleep, had the most wonderful dreams, and then when I woke up the crisis was completely over! Now, that's what I'm talking about!"

It looked like we had the milk to thank. I wondered, though, how long the effects would last.

"So, did you bring me more?" he asked again, a hint of the pop idol's usual testiness creeping back into his voice.

I told him I hadn't, but that I could have some brought in when we were done talking.

"Oh, good," he said, relieved. "Good, good, good. Good-good, good-good, good."

"You wanted to see us?" I said, hoping to change the subject and wrap up the meeting before he could get mad again.

"Yes," Our Leader said. "To thank you. Have I yet?"

"Well, you asked how you *can* thank us, said that you *would* thank us, then asked if you *had* thanked us."

"Good!"

Scott stepped in. "Um, sir, with Victoria's, uh, departure, there is the question of the open Communications Director role..."

"Of course, of course! And I'm so proud you persevered through your demotion, Mr. Jones. You've definitely proved yourself loyal."

"So, you mean...?" Scott gibbered excitedly.

"Which one of you came up with that Hero Pup song?"

"What?" asked Scott.

He sang it operatically: "'Violet, the Hero Pup! Don't cross her, or she'll *ruff* you up!' Brilliant."

Debbie looked up from her phone. "I did," she said brightly. She glanced at me nervously. "Though the original idea of the naming contest was..."

"It was all Debbie," I affirmed. She smiled at me with warm surprise.

Our Leader grinned. "Well, if you can make a snarling

robot beast popular, I can only imagine what you can do for this suave, yet lately under-appreciated, king."

"President," I corrected.

Ignoring me, he told Debbie, "Looks like we've found our next Comms Director!"

She lit up like a cellphone. "Hashtag #blessed!" she chirped. "OMG, I have to wooze about this right away."

"Booze about this?" Our Leader asked with some wonder. He picked up a half-filled bottle that had been idling by the lion feet of his throne. "Sorry, but all I have is this bubbly pink Moscato from New Year's. It's probably flat and a little warm, but I guess beggars can't be choosers."

A chill ran down my spine as the President brought the bottle's glass mouth to his. What if that was the bottle Victoria had poisoned at the party? Rushing forward, I shrieked, "No, wait!"

Our Leader laughed boisterously. "Well, isn't Hamner the little boozehound! OK, you may have it. Looks like you need it more than me."

I grabbed it before he could change his mind. Turning back to the team, I noticed Scott looking glum. He wasn't taking well the news that he wouldn't be getting his old job back. Patting my colleague on the back, I said, "Mr. President? I think Scott should be the new Crisis Communications Manager."

Our Leader's jaw flung wide. Debbie dropped her phone. Scott stammered, "B-but, that's your job."

"It's a good time for me to step away," I explained. To Scott, I whispered, "Anyway, you don't really want to take photographs of Our Leader eating ice cream for your entire career, do you?"

"But without you, how will I—?"

"Without *me*? Without *you*, Maria and I would still be locked up in Joe Steele's penthouse. You're going to do great."

Scott looked touched. "Thanks, man."

Our Leader's face looked all screwed up, as if he'd just heard me farting. His expression turned blank for many more long seconds. I wasn't sure what he was going to do. He might let me go, or he might have the guards send me to a dungeon that actually does exist. Each seemed equally possible.

"Ham-ham..." Our Leader whined pitifully. "I'm... I'm really going to *miss* you."

There was a long awkward pause. I wondered if I should hug him.

"What are you...what are you going to do?" he wanted to know.

"I'm going to start my own PR consultancy," I announced with a confidence that surprised even me.

His eyes lit up. "So, we could still...consult you occasionally?"

Heck no, I thought. "Maybe, if things work out," I said.

"Oh, that's *very* exciting," he said, happy again. "Hamner PR, eh? The *n* is silent?"

"Actually," I said, "I was thinking of calling it *Utopia PR*."

For Althea.

"Ooh, very cynical, I like that." Our Leader winked. "Well, I wish you the very best. You've done wonderful work for me Blake. Wonderful, wonderful, wonderful..."

His eyes lingered on an empty bowl that lay overturned on the floor.

"Hugs?" I offered.

"Hugs!" he returned, pulling me in.

Debbie snapped a picture on her phone, presumably for social.

Our Leader tightened his grip around my shoulders. Signaling to Scott, I pointed at the empty cereal bowl and mouthed the words, "Go! Now!"

Maria helped me gather up my things from the office. Before leaving the Compound, I called one last meeting with the PR team—what was left of it—in the Comms Situation Room. Debbie surprised me with a pink box labeled DONUTS.

"Oh wow!" I said, lifting the lid. To my dismay, it was packed full of rainbow-striped sand, like a kid's arts-and-crafts project.

"They've been trending," explained our social media expert, beaming. "Zand just opened a bakery. Straw?"

"You know, that looks great, but Maria really has been on my back to cut out the desserts," I said. "But please, go ahead and eat."

Shrugging, she grabbed a straw and leaned forward into the box. Hesitating, she asked, "Through the nose or the mouth, you think?"

Scott and I answered simultaneously.

She looked confused. "No-zouth?"

I punched Scott, then replied, "Mouth! Please, please do not snort that."

Debbie took a slurp and came up gasping for air. "Wow! I didn't think it would be so moist!"

I gagged.

"Guess it really is a paste-ry. Get it? Paste?" Scott joked.

"Enough!" I roared. "I called you here for a final meeting because I had a couple of ideas and didn't want to leave you guys hanging before I left the job. We got through the crisis, yes, but there are a couple more things you can do to make sure it sticks. First, you'll need to resurrect Violet. People love a good second coming."

"Ooh, that could go viral," said Debbie. "Hashtag #VioletReborn. Hm, do you think should we wait for Easter?"

"Like where your head's at, but no, do it now—sooner the better. Next, you're going to need to convince Our Leader to go on a speaking tour to reconnect with the people. To remind everyone why they voted for him. Also, it might keep him from coming up with crazy new policies for a while."

Scott looked unsure. "He doesn't love giving speeches."

"Pitch it to him as a singing tour, but he has to talk to the audience between songs."

Debbie's eyes lit up. "Violet could open for him!"

I wasn't quite sure how that would work, but Debbie had been pretty on-point with the Hero Pup thing so far, so I said, "Yeah, sure, but let Our Leader sing the theme song."

"Oh, good idea," she said. "He'll love that."

I grabbed my coat from the round table and headed for the door.

Scott thrust out his hand to shake. "Best of luck, my friend."

I thanked him, but the truth was I didn't feel like I needed luck. For the first time in a long time, I felt in control of my destiny.

Maria's eyes bulged when I returned to my office to collect the last few boxes. My first instinct, naturally, was to go into crisis mode. "What did you find?" I demanded, wracking my brain for what embarrassingly lewd gift from Scott she might have discovered while cleaning.

"I just got a call from a travel agent to go over our itinerary," she said.

I blinked. "Were we planning a trip?"

She held up her arms in disbelief. "Remember when Joe Steele said he was going to send us on our honeymoon in exchange for keeping quiet?"

I paused. "Yeah?"

"Well, turns out he booked it. An all-expenses-paid, three-month trip to an island resort! He must have done it before the rally, and I guess he never had a chance to cancel it."

It felt like being knocked over by a feather. "What did you tell the travel agent?"

"I, um...well, she went over the itinerary," she said with a shrug, "and I replied, 'That sounds great.' Then, she said she'd e-mail over the boarding tickets and hotel confirmation."

"And you said?"

"I said, 'Great, thanks.'"

"I love you." I thought about it some more. "Yeah, I don't think I feel bad about this."

Maria hesitated, then nodded. "Me, neither."

CHAPTER
THIRTY-TWO

T HE ISLAND SUN rendered our white linen curtains ineffectual, but I was getting used to this after two months in paradise. I could comfortably sleep in until about ten.

My wife wasn't in bed, so with a deep breath, I sat up and swung my feet onto the bamboo floor. My first instinct was to check the back porch. Sure enough, I found Maria lounging luxuriantly in a wooden recliner. Her chocolate skin and tangerine bikini glowed tantalizingly through a lacy cover-up. She was gazing through a pair of sunglasses at the azure ocean, but when I approached, she tilted her head back to look at me upside-down. "What do *you* want?"

"Thanks for letting me sleep in."

She grinned. "Maybe there's something you can do for me in return."

That got me a little tingly. All casual, I replied, "Oh?"

"Breakfast," she said with a wink. "One of those coconut yogurt shakes from the juice bar in town."

I chuckled. She practically had an addiction to those things. "Sure, want to go now?"

Maria wrinkled her nose. "No, my stomach's been a little weird this morning. Lying here in the sun is helping, so...I was hoping..."

"I'll go and bring some back."

She tipped down her shades and smiled. "You do love me."

I smirked. "Maybe there's something you can do for me in return."

"Maybe," said Maria, flashing her tongue. She tugged gently on one of the natural curls she had welcomed back into her hair since leaving her job at Triple N.

I put on a tropical shirt and some swim trunks, because here it was always good to be ready for a swim. As I slipped on a pair of soft leather sandals, I asked if she wanted me to pick up any medicine for her stomach. "Or, do you think it's still just the withdrawal?"

Maria had quit vaping the day we arrived at the resort. We'd both made resolutions, actually. I'd really cut back on the sweets and was even drinking my coffee black! The cabin had a kitchenette, so I'd started cooking again. I had picked up some great new island recipes, like mango chicken and pineapple shrimp. It was working, too. The clothes I'd brought from home looked a little baggy on me now.

"No, I'll be fine," she said. "I don't know what it is, but the sun's doing me good."

As I was leaving, Maria asked, "Ham? How would you pitch this place?"

I smiled ear to ear. "Better than any hologram."

I didn't mind going into town. It was a nice stroll through the palms. You could tell it was going to be another hot day, but a gentle breeze offered some relief. Maybe after breakfast we'd go swimming, if Maria was up for it.

The town was really just a single street, with restaurants and gift shops interspersed between grand entrances to the various resorts. Thanks to that Woozle money, we were staying at the place with arguably the grandest entrance. The gate consisted of two golden elephants standing on their hind legs and linking trunks to form an arch. I wondered if they actually did that.

I jumped as a man in a flowery button-down materialized out of nowhere. He could've given Debbie a run for her money. "Sea-Doo?" he asked.

"Not today," I said, quickly moving past him.

Actually, I had to appreciate the simplicity of the marketing. How many things could be sold on a single recitation of its two-syllable name? Just hearing "Sea-Doo" conjured images of speeding through a foamy blue ocean with my lady's hands locked around my muscular, non-fatty waist.

There was a long line for the shake shack, as usual. That was one problem with sleeping in.

Oh well, I thought. I'd faced greater crises.

The man and woman in front of me were engaged in a fairly serious-looking conversation, considering we were in paradise. They were both formally dressed and wore name tags from one of the other resorts.

"Maybe it was the mango?" said the woman.

"This is a disaster," said the man.

"The papaya, perhaps?"

"It doesn't matter," he replied. "We've already had three early departures, and the other guests want answers. What are we going to do?"

I cleared my throat. When they turned to look, I said, "Hi, sorry, but I couldn't help but overhear your conversation. My name is Blake Hamner. That's H-a-m-n-e-r: the *n* is silent. Anyway, I'm a PR crisis specialist, and I think I might have a couple ideas for you on how to smooth things over for your guests..."

I handed them a card freshly printed in our hotel's business center. It read *Utopia PR* in calming light-blue lettering.

"If you're game, I could meet you for lunch to talk over your situation. No charge unless I give you an idea that works, though I've got to warn you right now that I most certainly will."

I thought they were going to kiss me. I could have kissed me, too.

I was feeling so good about myself when I reached the counter that I elected to add an energy-vitamin boost to my breakfast shake.

As I turned around with my two big drinks, someone yelped my name. To my surprise, standing at the end of the line with a big grin on his face was Rico Fuentes, former Press Secretary to Our Leader. He was wearing a somewhat threatening T-shirt that read, *Slice and Paradise*. I didn't know what to make of it, let alone him, so I asked, "What are you doing here?"

"Getting a coconut milk. I can't get enough of 'em."

"No, I mean, what are you doing on the island?"

"Oh! Well..." He beckoned me closer and whispered into my ear, "I got sent here for rehab."

I took a step back. "I see."

"Pretty sweet, right?" he asked. "I've never felt so chilled out, you know? I'm thinking about renting a Sea-

Doo. Oh hey, did you hear Scott's getting married to Chief Overseer Mel Copps?"

I nodded. "Hard to believe he's finally settling down."

Rico held out his hands in astonishment. "When did they even meet?"

"Oh, I guess you weren't around for that, huh?"

"Oh," pouted Rico, and I saw a flash of his old morose self. "I really missed a lot, didn't I?"

Part of me wanted to ask where they'd been keeping him before they shipped him here, but I decided I'd rather get back to my wife.

"So, anyway," I said, looking over his shoulder to plot my exit. "Maybe we'll see you around."

His eyes lit up. "Is Maria here with you?"

I nodded.

"How long you guys in town?"

"Another month."

"Wow, cool! And then what? You quit your job, right?"

"Right, but I'm starting up my own PR shop."

"Right on!" he enthused. "And Maria? She going back to Triple N?"

I shook my head. "She's got something, but I can't go into details yet."

Actually, no one had told me to keep it a secret, but the shakes were melting. "So great seeing you," I said, stepping away.

Another reason I didn't mind going out for shakes was that we were still celebrating Maria's big career news.

Pretty much as soon as Joe Steele went to jail, Triple N sent some people to find us here at the resort. They told her they'd made a huge mistake firing her and begged her to come back. They said she could have any time slot she wanted.

The sudden change in heart got me suspicious, so I called Debbie to check on Maria's social score. Turned out, the piece we shot at the Compound had shown that it was Maria Worthington—not the Triple N brand—who was the most trusted name in news. Maria brought this to the attention of the network scouts. Then she told them to leave.

Maria called up her agent and asked if she could get a new show on a competitive news network. She wanted full control—it would have to be all info, no 'tainment. Well, maybe a little 'tainment—it *was* television. But certainly no *Splash-Q*.

Maria's agent set up a few casual phone calls that soon turned into more serious negotiations. Before we could even wrap our heads around the possibility of this crazy idea becoming a reality, my wife received a contract by e-mail from the Public Broadcasting Network.

I guess I wasn't so surprised. That was Maria.

I knocked playfully on the door to our cabana. "Room service."

She didn't answer, so I knocked again. "Oh, Miss? I've got something juicy for you."

She still didn't come to the door, so I let myself in. I figured she'd fallen asleep in the lounge chair again.

I didn't see her out back when I looked through the glass door. "Maria?"

A moan came from the bathroom. "I'm in here."

I put down the drinks and went to the door. "Are you OK?"

She tipped open the door, releasing a sour smell into my nostrils. The weird thing was that she looked happy.

"Did you throw up?!" I asked with alarm, falling instantly into crisis mode.

Maria's perplexing grin grew.

"What's going on?" I demanded.

"Come for your honeymoon, stay for your baby-moon!" exclaimed my wife, wiping her face with a towel. "How's *that* for a pitch?"

My job's always been to craft the right response to everything. Maria remains the only person who knows how to leave me speechless.

ABOUT
THE AUTHOR

ADAM BENDER is an award-winning journalist and author of speculative fiction that explores modern-day societal fears with a mix of action, romance and humor.

Bender's latest novel is *Utopia PR*, a speculative satire about a public-relations specialist who struggles to find work-life balance while managing crisis after crisis for a dystopian American president.

Previously, Bender wrote *The Wanderer and the New West*, a near-future western about a rogue vigilante who seeks redemption in a lawless America that fully protects the rights of armed citizens to stand their ground. Named to *Kirkus Reviews'* Best Books of 2018, the novel also won gold for Dystopia in the 2018 Readers' Favorite Awards and best Western Fiction in the 2018 National Indie Excellence Awards.

Bender authored *We, The Watched* and *Divided We Fall* in a dystopian series about an amnesiac who struggles to conform in a surveillance society where the government keeps a Watched list of its own citizens. Also, Bender has published several short stories.

In his day job as a journalist, Bender covers telecom and internet regulation for *Communications Daily*. He has won awards for his reporting from the Society of Professional Journalists, the Specialized Information Publishers Association, and the Society for Advancing Business Editing and Writing.

Bender lives in Philadelphia with his wife Mallika and son Rishi. He's usually a rather modest and amiable fellow.

Learn more about the author at WatchAdam.blog and join *The Underground* email newsletter for news and info on Adam Bender's latest projects. Follow him on Facebook (wethewatched) and @WatchAdam on Twitter and Instagram.

WE, THE WATCHED

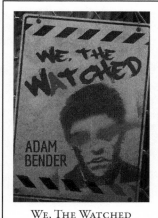

WE, THE WATCHED

An amnesiac struggles to conform in a surveillance society in the novel acclaimed by *Kirkus Reviews* as "a page-turner of the highest order" and a "deeply allegorical and powerfully thought-provoking dystopian must-read."

Seven wakes in a forest outside the capital of a nation he doesn't recognize. When he enters the city, he discovers a surveillance society with no separation between Church and State. The government keeps a Watched list of its own citizens and deploys a police force called the Guard to sniff out Heretics. While Seven's blank-slate perspective lets him see through the government's propaganda, he soon draws the eyes of the Guard.

Now available as a paperback and eBook! For more information, visit WeTheWatched.com.

DIVIDED WE FALL

A totalitarian government orders Agent Eve Parker to arrest her fiancé when he becomes a revolutionary known as Seven. When Eve learns more about the President's plan to broaden citizen surveillance, she begins to question if she's on the right side. Meanwhile, a foreign enemy threatens to take advantage of an increasingly divided nation.

DIVIDED WE FALL

The sequel to *We, The Watched* "raises interesting questions about the influence of propaganda on the construction of the self, the idea of true tabula rasa and the power of memory," says *Publishers Weekly*. "The central love story propels the narrative energetically."

"Bender's sequel is a worthy delivery on the promise of his riveting debut," says *Kirkus Reviews*. "A novel about a scheming president offers an excellent read for those who love thrillers or 21st-century history."

Now available as a paperback and eBook! For more information, visit WeTheDivided.com.

THE WANDERER AND THE
NEW WEST

A rogue vigilante seeks redemption in a lawless, near-future America that fully protects the rights of armed citizens to stand their ground.

When a marksman known as the Wanderer opens war against injustice in the state of Arizona, his violent actions attract the attention of journalist Rosa Veras, writer of a subversive blog about America's return to the Wild West.

Named to *Kirkus Reviews'* Best Books of 2018, *The Wanderer and the New West* won gold for Dystopia in the 2018 Readers' Favorite Awards and best Western Fiction in the 2018 National Indie Excellence Awards.

"A dystopian novel about an America ruled by gangs and gun manufacturers and about the brave few who are willing to fight them both," says *Kirkus Reviews*. "A tight, thoughtful work that has much to offer readers on both sides of the gun control debate."

Now available as a paperback, eBook and audiobook! For more information, visit WhoIsTheWanderer.com.